BENEATH
THE SWIMMING POOLS, THE
TEETH!

MARK JASKOWSKI

WEIRD
PUNK

Copyright © 2025 by Mark Jaskowski, Artists, Weirdpunk Books

First Edition

WP-0029

Print ISBN 978-1-951658-49-6

Cover art by Sam Richard

Editing and internal layout/formatting by Sam Richard

Weirdpunk Books logos by Ira Rat

Weirdpunk Books

www.weirdpunkbooks.com

CONTENTS

––––––––––

BACK WHEN MY SKIN STILL LOOKED AND FELT LIKE skin, I met up with a guy it's not a good sign to meet up with and he didn't really offer me a job, but he did say he'd heard a bit about me from our mutual friend and all his questions circled around how I didn't have any money and didn't I go to college and how did all that happen, positioning him as the grown-up with each one, and I guess I came back a little firmer than I thought about that because Alex started giving me the self-help eyes, the look that's all about how there's plenty of money if you want to make it.

And I guess this might have all come from his watching me when I was pretty sure he hadn't, while I was clocking how thick the folded stack of twenties he'd pulled out of his wallet was. Maybe two months before. We were in Trevor's car on the way back from a downtown bar some nothing night, shortly after Trevor got stabbed and got sober, in whatever order those things happened, and then resurfaced a little bit later, neither having stuck. We were stopped at the gas station to pick up some PBR and Trevor didn't have any money. I shrugged about how I'd made that confession fucking hours ago and Alex pulled his wallet and it wasn't until that moment that I considered that maybe his wardrobe, like the shiny maroon shirt and gray pants he'd worn to the bar, might not be a poserish attempt to curry respect from those of us who didn't know any better but rather something like the current style.

I was in the backseat and it was Trevor's car so though my first thought was of how I might find a way to pocket the cash he tucked back into his billfold and the center console after peeling off a little for the beer and gas—the trick wouldn't be getting past Alex for the grab but Trevor—I let that thought go quick. Alex scared me, actually, in how he stood out from Trevor's opioid friends, the things I had begun to suspect he may have done toward that end.

I wondered what he did for a job, for one, whether some of the bullshit stories I'd heard him tell at parties—strip clubs with clients and bosses, drugged-out encounters in expensive hotels, gambling around cigars—were less bullshit than I had thought and whether that was calculated as well: let it all ring false except for the money, and let the listener figure it out from there.

But I was sure he hadn't seen me tracking his

money. Then again, the only reason to pull that much out in company is to draw eyes.

In any event, two months later, he made me say it: "So, where do you work?"

He sat back like this was an unexpected question. "Are you looking for a job, man?"

"Of course."

"It's a little office. We're hiring, if you'd like to come in."

It didn't bother me until later how he'd avoided telling me the name of the company, certainly until after I'd driven out toward Maitland, turning off the state road into the lot of an office park, parked and climbed the stairs in my best approximation of business-casual to an unmarked-but-for-a-number door that looked unoccupied until I entered.

His eyes would glide off mine, though they made contact, like we'd never seen each other. It was not my first warning sign, though, after the unmarked door and the waiting room with no logos or pamphlets, the weirdly buzzing cubicle back room through a short hallway. All the unmarked colorless walls made the place feel like it would have looked just the same the day before this particular shingle was hung and would be returned to that state the day after they closed up.

Then, sitting in an uncomfortable chair with three other unlikely candidates for entry-level office work and waiting for the opportunity to fill out the same forms they were, my eyes slid right off Alex's with none of the stick of recognition as he passed by the narrow hallway opening, and the clerk called me over and told me she'd need my driver's license and social security and signature on the dotted squares of the last page.

I carried the packet back to the chair with me and took a ball-point pen from a coffee cup to tap like I was thinking about my answers, while I was weighing working for a cold-call scam operation.

It wasn't that I was necessarily averse to committing some organized fraud right then, but they wanted photocopies of all my ID. I was pretty sure Alex's wouldn't be on file, nor anyone else with cash like his, so I waited for the clerk to turn around to dig in a filing cabinet and rolled the hired-on-the-spot application packet up and stuck it in my back pocket as I left.

It could have been the end of the whole thing.

But at a party the next weekend, which I only agreed to go to because I was even more broke than the week before and some parties have kegs and bottles and other things, along with a pleasant sort of anonymity if you're up for keeping to small talk the whole night. These all sounded pretty fucking good so I showed with Mike, that home-nurse friend of Trevor's, and we wandered into a house I'd never been in before but may as well have.

Rock-band tee shirts and thrift-store skirts, jeans and tights moving over management-company carpet and sitting on the arms of occupied chairs and pouring liquor into plastic cups in the kitchen. A move-in-move-out apartment on the edge of the

----

college's reach, suitable for part-time drug dealers as much as working students and for the same reasons, but this crowd was a little older than I might have expected.

I wandered the rooms allotted to the party and mingled as best I could, funneling spiced rum down my throat until my teeth tasted like caramel and vanilla, and ran into Mike in the kitchen and we laughed about finding ourselves in a place like this, then laughed again and louder at how much we'd been enjoying ourselves, and I settled my head back down after throwing it back and saw over Mike's shoulder Alex, whom I'd last seen in a shitty office in shiny dress clothes, now dressed in an AC/DC shirt tucked into light blue jeans talking to a group of girls who looked like they could be his nieces.

Then he patted one on the head and another somewhere else and peeled off, turning his torso so he could talk to someone else while keeping his legs planted in the conversation circle. His new friend looked familiar, like maybe I knew him when we were kids, before he grew into this lanky guy with big hands and a thin smile that never left his face but didn't ever reach his eyes.

They talked for a short while, Alex's mouth up to this vaguely familiar guy's ear, until they came to some kind of an agreement and Alex looked back toward his girls, not at them but between their heads at the partiers, and said just loud enough to be heard, "Anybody feel like some weed?"

He and the familiar guy raised their hands, acknowledging the cheers from the assembled, and sauntered out the front door and into an ancient green sedan. Mike and I followed in their wake, through a sea of cooling enthusiasm—not like the partiers weren't excited about a little haze on their evening, just like they were going to wait until they were breathing it in before they got worked up about it—onto the front porch. We found a couple plastic chairs to the side of all the people and parked ourselves.

Mike offered me my first cigarette in three or four months and I took it, sparked and breathed in and breathed out and felt myself doing the same satisfied face I'd seen on every smoker who thought they'd quit I ever bummed one to, and Mike and I sat and puffed until a white panel van squealed to a stop and let loose Alex and his familiar friend and the friend shouted, "Hey hey, we got the fucking ex!" They trotted up the front steps like conquering heroes and Alex's eyes met mine and they stuck this time. He spun around like he was going to tell me something but instead just held his hands out to his sides walking backwards and grinned and turned back around into the party.

Mike gave me a look and I'm pretty sure my face looked just the same. There's a line stretching out from that moment in my memory, one where he and I do what we would normally have done when we saw some guys come back from a drug buy with a different

drug than they went out for and in a different vehicle:
recognize a bad fucking scene and mosey along. I
imagine, in that version, we would have gone about
our night, feeling it a pretty big loss at the time but
thinking of it later as a minor amusement if we
remembered it at all.

I guess Mike would have been fine, all things
considered. He had a job he liked. Some debt, but the
nursing-school kind, nothing he wouldn't have
managed over time. Me, I don't know how I would
have wound up, but sometimes I think it could have
turned out pretty good. That I would have figured
myself out.

But events have their own momentum, their own
patterns, and it can feel good to give into them, so
what we did was shrug about how things go sometimes and let the cheap cocktails we'd been swigging
show in our smiles and swayed back inside. I was
having a pleasant night in spite of myself, and I
wondered how Alex was going to take my presence,
whether he'd acknowledge my appearance at his
office, so I made the rounds through newly revitalized
partiers until the crowd around him faded a little and
sidled up and said hi.

He looked right in my eyes and made his face light
up a little like I was an old friend he was surprised to
see again, and did it convincingly enough that I could
see falling for it if things were different.

"Hey hey, Dusty! Been a while."

I didn't mention that it hadn't been that long.

"Well, hell, I thought that might have been you outside. Don't see you around usually."

"You know, slow night. Thought I'd see what I could see."

"And who, right?"

This didn't really make sense to me. I looked over his shoulder and saw Mike tossing his head back like a baby bird and lowering a dose of the new ex into his mouth, and that didn't really make sense, either.

Alex went to walk away and did a little Columbo turn, like he was just remembering something. "Say, are you still looking for a job? Because I think I might have something."

I shrugged a maybe and then saw he looked serious and nodded, figuring he'd give me another anonymous office to go to in another office park, or maybe the same one again. Maybe he'd have a little something for me to deliver, or a little favor to ask like they did in the better country songs, but he had something a little more immediate in mind, and it's not that I didn't know better, hadn't seen the van pull up and Mike swallow himself into the clouds and a little office that could hardly pretend to put out as much money as my man carried.

No, I knew all this and remembered it. I just really did need some fucking money.

I felt something happening. Perhaps it would be something good.

Alex took me out to the back and pointed out a couple groups of people—standing around the fire pit

----

and sitting all around the glass patio table—who wouldn't be interested in talking to him, let alone buying, and handed me a large baggie stuffed with smaller baggies for a distribution and sales opportunity I was about to prove rather upsettingly adept at.

"Keep the big one open in your pocket and reach in for what you need. People see how much you have left, it helps them start calculating whether it's worth it to try to jump you."

I nodded fast, like of course I knew this and it was a little condescending to think he had to tell me, and Alex sped through the rest to accommodate. I headed outside and found that there was another advantage: every time I reached into my pocket to pull out a new bag it slowed the sale a little, so that the circle around me grew into a nice ring of new friends.

I got rid of the little bags inside of the big bag and held my hands out to my sides, doing all but pulling out my pockets and sticking out my lower lip, so the remnants of my crowd dispersed and set to divvying up and dosing, and headed back inside.

Alex was leaning against the kitchen bar and grinning at people when I sidled up and asked if there was any more. He just whistled and clapped his hand on my shoulder and said no, that was all of it, and he knew he could count on me.

"That's enough to feed the whole house, if they pass it around."

I passed him my pocketful of money. I hadn't

counted it or put it in any kind of order. He tapped it into shape and flipped through and frowned.

"What's it, low?"

"No, it's high."

He looked at me and I looked at him and he laughed and I smiled about how it's one of those things. He peeled me off something like a quarter of the haul, a little higher than I'd expected, and watched me tuck it into my pocket.

"A little better opening this time, huh?" and, waving off my protest, "No, it's just nice to know who's up for some work now and then."

He pulled one last little baggie out of his pocket with the pills crushed up at the bottom, like a special magic trick, and passed it to me. I had no intention of taking it, but gestures require responses to complete themselves and I was compelled to put my hand out before I was compelled to think, and then the plastic was between my fingers and moving to my pocket.

"Enough work for one night, don't you think?" he said, looking around at the blurrier tenor the apartment had taken. "Everyone else is blasting off. I'm not about to get left behind."

He had that look on his face that a certain kind person gets very good at deploying when they get a sense that you'd like to avoid the awkwardness of saying no, and I could see it happening in real time, but I was already committed to going along.

So when I pinched some out of the bag I did it so he couldn't see how there was nothing between my

----

finger and my thumb. When he did the same, I couldn't see it, either, so we each either did or didn't take a pinch of what turned out to not be the good stuff, quite.

And all around, the partygoers tuned into the new frequency the party was buzzing at and someone turned up the stereo in the living room to a strong strain of electronic drums and fuzzy distortion and Alex faded away while I wasn't looking. I whipped my head around and caught a dirty-blond buzz cut and a white strip of neck and a black tee shirt and he was gone.

I picked up my plastic cup and scanned the now-disorganized kitchen bar, bottles of booze and soda and juice strewn across all the sticky surfaces, and figured that maybe SoCo and lime would be tolerable if I lengthened it out with club soda. The whiskey had all been shot and the bottles left were mostly good for a sugar high. I went ahead and threw one together and it felt pretty good going down, enough that I mixed another before I went to take a look around.

Whoever put the music on was grooving to it, much slower than the desperate-to-fuck pace that that usually gets called up at that time of night, along with ten or so of their new best friends. They moved slowly and looked, for the most part, toward the ceiling. The hallway was lined with partiers who had had enough, slumped down and conked out on the way to the bathroom, where five people were ignoring the one sitting to piss because they'd filled the tub and cut an empty two-liter of Sierra Mist in half across its waist and stuffed the mouth with mesh faucet filters from the hardware store and the wire filters with weed they don't seem to have needed Alex for after all, and I propped myself against the door frame and watched one of them get a lighter going and touch the flame to the ground-up bud until it caught enough, and the smoker pulled hard and a third person pushed the bottle down into the water and the smoker's eyes bugged out and he slumped against the wall streaming smoke out of a huge smile.

It had been a long time since I'd seen a proper homemade gravity bong, and the effects of it—the eyes rolling back, the general loss of mobility in the hands and the face—and I was settled in to watch the next round when I felt something similar get started on the back of my neck.

I scrambled back and took a couple strong pulls on my fizzy bullshit cocktail, which was cold, which helped at first, but then the feeling at the back of my skull bloomed into blurry waves and I stared into my red cup and realized what I should have had figured from the moment I met Alex.

And then some other shit happened, most likely.

And then I woke up.

– – – – – – – – –

Plastic ridges of the bed of a pickup truck had been digging into my flesh for hours. Not enough hours, judging from how my eyelids gripped my eyeballs like gummy sandpaper, but when I pulled myself up to roll over, I could feel strips of compressed flesh pushing themselves back into shape, waking up every painful nerve ending on the way.

Once I got myself up to sitting and had a sunbleached view of the chipped blue paint of the lip of the bed and the detritus in the cab I figured it was something, at least, that I had crawled back to my own truck.

And I remembered hazily:

Stumbling from wall to wall, trying to stay vertical. No one standing in my eyeline but it doesn't feel like the room is empty. Like I'm pushing through a crowd I can't see until I find the front door...

Blinking and squinting didn't bring up any more

of the flash of memory, so I set to the stiff and difficult work of getting myself up and out of the truck bed, until my feet found the asphalt and my ankles and then knees cracked out their protest but held, and I hauled myself into the driver's seat and twisted around until my back cracked into something like its usual alignment and made my breath a little freer and my eyesight a little clearer until I could tell that I was on the same street I had parked on, a block or so from the party house.

My stomach settled a little with that familiarity, but my temper didn't—it was the same place something went wrong, and while perhaps it couldn't have gone all that wrong if I slept it off in back of my own truck, I did have the gap in my memory and real uncomfortableness around what I could remember from the last moments before my broadcast went fuzzy.

I looked around the car for a half-drunk coffee or maybe the dregs of a Gatorade, but of course there was nothing, so I swallowed as hard as I could into my dry throat, which was unsuccessful and required some intense work from muscles I don't think I'd ever thought about before, and drove real slow past the party house.

One car shared the driveway with the white van, and there was nothing to suggest that a rager got dark there last night; no debris in the lawn, no cars in front of the house, nobody passed out in the lawn chairs and love seat on the porch. Nothing looked broken or stolen, nothing suggested anyone other than a responsible neighbor lived there, and as I passed the driveway the picture shimmered a bit, like a dirty recording shined through the perfect façade in crackling tape distortion I tried to blink away like the hangover symptom I assumed it was, and I pulled into the complex network of subdivision arteries to a road I at least knew the name of and drove until I found a place that would sell me beef and cheese in a bun with a huge plastic cup of lemonade so I could panic a minute at the first window until I checked the glovebox and found my wallet under the owner's manual and envelopes from an old party-prep reflex. The burgers didn't help as much as they used to but the lemonade got my throat working and some saliva moving so I regrouped a little to drive home and sleep until my phone buzzed me awake with Mike asking me what the fuck happened and I rolled over and ignored it and sweated salt in a daze.

Eventually I had to let Mike know I was alive, which would normally have been something I did semi-automatically, moving my thumbs before my brain came online, but something was pulling there hard, tugging the rest of my body into sludge until even driving to the hookah-and-coffee place the next day felt like an ordeal, and my feet were like sponges walking to the patio table where Mike was waiting. Maybe this was the ex comedown—I'd heard plenty about how that could feel a lot like a severe depression, or create one—but it was different than I'd imagined it.

Mike had a honey latte and an IPA in a bottle and was alternating sips from each. He kept doing it until I was convinced it was really on purpose, despite how I could smell both and pretty clearly imagine what he was doing to himself. It was a busy evening but not quite to the busy part yet, so enough people were working that one came out with only coffee, which I held up near my nose.

"I think my sense of smell is all fucked up," Mike said over his most recent sip of beer was down. "Kinda the least of my discomforts, I guess, but it turns out these work pretty well," and he slurped some honey-coffee foam off the top of his cup, then licked some off his stubble. "Glad to see you didn't wind up dead in a bathroom man. I was worried for a minute."

"It got pretty wild, huh?"

"Yeah," running his thumb around the rim of his coffee cup, "I guess it did, but I'm a little hazy on… well, a lot of it."

I took down the rest of my coffee to try to steady myself a little more before we started comparing notes, starting with how I was pretty sure Alex slipped me a heavy dose of something fucking weird, which would suggest that what I'd been passing around was pretty daffy, too. Mike looked a little embarrassed because it turned out his picture fizzed out a bit before mine—when we decided to stay and see where the evening took us, he'd hoisted his sail quick. Neither of us could put together much about what happened in the living room after the music got loud, but Mike looked like he had the same pull in his brain as I did, toward a gap in his memory that was more pressing than your average Saturday-night blackout.

So we talked a bit more and agreed to see if we could find anything out but also that it would be best to be subtle, certainly not leaving any digital paper trails, and a few days later I had to go back to work, not wanting to call out more than one day on what still felt wrong with me.

––––––––

Four hours into the workday wasn't as bad as it sounds, once I got past the first store. It was a chain-wide endcap strategy at every location so I was driving from store to store helping the store workers set up cardboard displays of batteries from the company that hired the company I worked for, the latest in a series of shit assignments that paid half-time for your drive but did provide plenty of drive time to try and balance your body chemistry, on days that was a concern, but my mistake came at the first place. I'd rushed in on a coffee and half a bagel I left in its paper on the passenger seat, figuring I'd grit my way through, but barely halfway through loading the batteries onto the paperboard display we'd folded the pieces of and assembled, the three workers I was assisting were shifting from sneaking glances at me to almost-openly staring. Not that I could really blame them—I could feel myself getting paler and sweatier, until I faked a phone call and came back saying it was the office, making sure I remembered to remind them to block the shelves every two hours. I put a little tang in my voice that they all picked up on and didn't quite hide their smirks. It was enough goodwill to get me through set-up and out the sliding door before my stomach finally started turning over. All the stores had full security-camera coverage down the four middle rows of the parking lot. I couldn't afford to be on tape hurling in front of customers, so I ran to the side of the building and let loose clinging to the brick corner, first in a thin stream and then a gush, and at the exact moment my nose and mouth were totally blocked, the anaerobic panic moment of every stomach virus that pushes you to think about death even if you weren't already, the pressure seemed to push up against some nerve and my tunnel vision squeezed down further and blurred in the middle and then blurred more until a shape emerged, like I was looking at a mountain or some kind of giant fang at a considerable distance and a clenching came over me and I coughed mid-stream and dropped to my hands and knees and started to get ready to be found dead there until the clench relaxed, leaving a soreness deep under my muscles and I spat and snorted out of the last stinging strands of it and rolled off to the side of my puddle and managed a sharp gasp as tears made my vision worse before finally bringing it back.

I looked around for the crowd that might have gathered, anyone rubbernecking on their way into the store, but I had pulled myself far enough away from the main flow that either nobody saw or no one felt like stopping to look. I pulled myself up and dusted my clothes off with my hand, or dusted the asphalt off my hands onto my clothes, and walked to my car and made sure to stop at a corner store for a mobile pharmacy of bottled drinks and over-the-counter pills on the way to the next store and this one a went little easier. It helped that I kept blinking hard, like the fluorescent lights were grating on me, which they always had before, but now they came down like distant suns. My eyes still itched, though, and blinking in those big blue-white rooms usually signaled you'd been working awhile, and the guys at that second store waved me aside and took over lifting the boxes. One even said, "Hey, they've got you working late, huh?" and all I had to do was blink some more and smile and shrug and that was it.

I got out that front door a bit smoother than I got out the last one, and then the one after that, too, and used my passenger-seat plastic-bag supplies to keep my keel more or less even through the next and then that was it, a full day of work that only added up to a sixty-five by the company math, plus a little bit for gas, and I got back to my apartment under the throbbing effects of my sugar/electrolyte/grease regimen, starving and bloated and nauseated all at once.

My bed was harder than usual, so I rolled around a bit to let it get comfortable but it never did. I got myself wedged against some pillows kind of on my side and thought it would work but my heart started pounding as soon as I'd been still for a couple minutes. My breathing grew shallow and my muscles got that itch for movement that maybe doesn't make you move but surely keeps you from sleeping.

I held myself down as long as I could, but my legs started to hurt like I'd been sitting in a stress position until I had to get up and move around even as my gut tossed and my face blanched, and I circled my apartment but the two species of sensation—the driving and the debilitating—didn't come into anything like a balance and so I got back in the car and drove around the neighborhood like I was going to find answers in my neighbors' parking spaces. These answers didn't come but the rumbling of the road was soothing, vibrations pulling my attention out from my body by pushing into it. I pulled around a few times and didn't feel like stopping so I drove to Mike's house, figuring comparing even empty notes would be something to do if it was only to confirm that someone else was living in this world with me, but no one answered my knock, or the second, or the third.

I was surely not up to kicking any doors in, so I tried the knob and the door swung open. I stood back and listened to the door hit the wall, its oval window rattling against the wood, and then the long silence that didn't really tell me anything at all. The place was ferociously cold and the rush of it locked me tense before I relaxed into it. It felt fantastic, chilled my stomach through my skin and cooled my blood until it pumped a little slower.

So Mike had been there recently, if he wasn't now, and his body was making similar demands as mine, but he'd gotten a bit further ahead of it than I had.

I worried briefly that I was going to feel better in a way that would push me toward laying down on the sofa and sleeping for a day or two, but the couple steps I took to keep that urge off negated it entirely and I started feeling better enough that I kept strolling through the little house—the rest of the living room, just in case Mike was behind some furniture or something; the bathroom with the glass shower door that would have classed the place up a bit if it wasn't an inch or two too short; the bedroom that served as a bedroom and the smaller one he kept a desk and a guitar in. I was pretty surprised by the second bedroom, and in this neighborhood, until I remembered that he had a job-type job, one that paid the bills all by itself, and could afford to live not extravagantly but very nearly by the standards of our circle: in possession of a bedroom that didn't have a bed in it. There were no people there, though, nothing out of the ordinary on a cursory glance, so I tried to think of places he might be on the way out the door. I hesitated a bit over whether I should lock the door before I closed it, but he'd left it unlocked when he left, I did the same before I went out to cruise some spots Mike might be, AC in the car dialed now all the way to meat-locker.

–––––––

THERE WAS NOBODY AT THE COFFEE-AND-HOOKAH BAR
where I first ran into Alex, except for the near-lifer
barista who reminded me of a running joke that
dated back to when I was in high school and told me I
was an embarrassment to my family as I carried the
coffee two sizes larger than I paid for out the door.
Nor was there anyone at a couple likely bars, though
it was only about five in the afternoon, so I drove
around a convoluted circle, into and out of parking
lots to roll slowly past the patios and peer into the
front windows. It was all a long shot, but I was feeling
a little better now that I knew to keep myself cool so I
felt like giving it a try for a while. Eventually the sun
touched the horizon and a familiar patio shone with
glare and the silhouettes of a couple friends I didn't
see as much of lately.

Megan, wearing low-rise jeans and a hoop belt
and most of a giant Misfits tee shirt, and her friend

and her black hoodie were all arranged in elaborate positions of poised reflection, signaling they were free for the night and getting ready for something. Megan saw me coming and swept her floppy pleather purse off the third chair and into her lap and sat up and motioned me to sit and started talking and before I knew it I was going to meet up with them somewhere with their usual crew, something about the new episode of a TV show and a party after.

"Mike gonna be there?"

"Man, I don't know, D. He usually is."

We chatted a bit more and I didn't know some of the people they mentioned, but it sounded like Trevor would be there, too, and that meant a solid enough platform for my presence, and maybe an appearance by Alex, whether that's what I wanted or not—an evening of chilled-out small talk and boozy political arguments with Trevor itself sounded pretty good—but then my skin started warming up and coming back to crawling and doing something that felt like sweating into my body, which put me right back on the main track, standing up to tell Megan and friend I was just dropping in for some iced tea and I'd meet them there, and up and into the shop for a large was truly fucking large and, even better, packed up to the top with ice that I pressed a fistful of to my forehead after slugging down half the tea back in the car while the AC struggled to work itself back up to speed. My skin calmed down where the ice touched and the water dripped, and the rest of it burned by comparison. The cup had started sweating and I wiped it across my face and put the car in gear and sped away, like the faster I drove and harder I sucked the rest of the tea the faster time would pass, and maybe jostle the world back into something resembling order.

Already I was starting to feel like I was watching myself from the outside, at the other end of a short tunnel with thick walls, bending and warping the light and grinding the smallest motions down to a twitching cluster of tics mimicking precision. I focused on the idea that it was all just hangover and rattled nerves and clenched my teeth down on top of that idea, trying to keep it in place. But my insides felt like they were stretching out and doubling back on themselves to fit in the same space but with more tension. Taffy growing white with the stretching.

I cruised around, trying to keep my speed within reason, and went out to a part of town I hadn't been to in a long time and realized I only really knew one house out there and got gas and was reminded of how bad rush hour can get even if you're on the surface roads you associate with days off when they're empty and made it to the party fashionably late if the starting time was for fashionably late, which it didn't appear to have been—everyone talking about the show they'd gathered to watch beforehand, which I gathered had to do with a bomb in a nursing home and a poison plant—so the introductions and haven't-seen-you-in-a-whiles came jumbled all on each other until I found Trevor and Megan at a table out back by the pool with some friends.

When I sat down I recognized them as some of Trevor's friends from high school, which seemed to point the night in a certain direction, and Trevor was sporting that even-all-around buzz-cut people seem to get the second or third time they decide that no, this isn't the moment for them to kick quite yet, but I didn't say anything. Who knew, maybe it was coming back in style, and anyway the sun was going down over the back neighbors' house and I was feeling good. Trevor passed me a cigarette and I let the conversation happen around me, about some egregious faux-pas committed by someone I didn't know. I nodded along with the beats of the story. They were easy enough to follow, to the point that I kind of stopped listening to the particulars, falling into the familiar rhythm of form without content. I stubbed my cigarette out on the lip of the coke can with a bit of water in the bottom and dropped it inside. A lull asserted itself over the conversation, the participants' grasping for the next story stretching into a moment to think about their stories and their audience and their personal histories, a moment into and through which charged a little parade from the sliding-glass door on its way to the pool, leaving a little trail of clothing and Solo cups on the concrete before a chorus of splashing, bare feet smearing around the remnants of the rain, leaching damp back into the air.

I turned too late for the leaping and just saw

Sebastian belly-deep in the shallow end, boxer shorts and nothing else, face up to the sky and one of the banana drinks Candace was blending inside sweating in a tall glass in his hand. Some more horsing around got started on the deck and Sebastian smiled and slugged on his drink such that little pieces of ice clacked against his teeth. Connor took a header into the pool halfway through a somersault he was trying out and Sebastian had the mouth of his glass turned toward him so the chlorinated water only went up his nose, not into his glass, and he grinned and quoted a movie. Candace came out with a new full blender in her hand and Sebastian clicked the rest of the ice against his teeth until no more liquid was forthcoming and set the glass down on the pool deck, where the frost bloomed and dripped a heavy ring of water around the base of the glass. My skin itched against the damp air, sucking against it without gaining anything, so I stood up and kicked off my boots and stripped off my jeans and sauntered over to the pool. I turned back, put my heels to the edge and made eye contact with my friends. Megan put her hand over a smile. Trevor raised his eyebrows. I crossed my hands over my chest and fell back into the water, breathing out slowly so I sank to the bottom, the swimming forms of the crew from inside wavering above me in a blur of porch light and bubbles and ass cheeks.

My lungs started to burn and I didn't want to climb through the people floating above me so I logrolled over a few times until I was clear and swam until my elbows bumped the corner of the floor and the wall and pushed up to the surface and took a long clear breath. Megan pulled on a cigarette so her face faded and flashed back into view. I couldn't see where Trevor had got to.

"You feel better?" Megan said.

"You know, I kind of fucking do."

I took a deep breath and sank down again, until my feet pushed against the floor of the pool, then my knees, then my tailbone. No one would mistake chlorine for salt, or a pool for the ocean, but I dug my toes against the plaster like it was sand, but halfway through the flexing the floor came loose just like sand and my toes were holding packs of it. I let go and looked down but the water wasn't even cloudy and stung my eyes.

I dug back in with my toes.

The divots from before held firm and then gave a little and then more and then something slashed at the pads of my toes. I flinched upward and turned into a somersault to look for the damage but there were no trails of blood, just a mess of white scratches. I couldn't see what made them and was suddenly too timid to try again, but I knew what it felt like I'd felt.

It was like several rows of razor-sharp teeth, waiting just under the surface.

I kicked out of my spin and came back up, to Megan still smoking like nothing had changed. I didn't know well enough to tell her it had, felt myself like I was teetering just on the edge of understanding something.

"Whose house is this?"

"It's mine. Hadn't you heard? I've got a pool and a fucking deck."

We laughed briefly, and I said, "No, but really, whose pool am I in?"

"Candace. I mean, Candace's mom."

I flexed my toes under the water but kept them pulled up far enough that there was no way they'd touch the floor, and looked over at Candace making the rounds with the pitcher of drinks, trying to switch my perception of her manner from life-of-the-party to active-and-welcoming-hostess, trying to see it through different eyes, but it still just looked like Candace. Sometimes context isn't everything.

Trevor's voice came in from around the corner of the house and Megan was watching me curiously enough that I started to feel weird just floating pants-less by myself so I pulled myself up over the lip, spending way more energy on the task than I remembered it requiring so my planned glistening emergence from the pool, onto one knee and then standing, was more like a damp flop onto my side and a roll onto my back with my shirt twisted all around my gut and chlorine dripping into my eyes, which flooded over in response and got me blinking until my eyes cleared and I was looking up at Megan and Trevor and, smiling over Trevor's shoulder, Alex.

‐ ‐ ‐ ‐ ‐ ‐

EVEN THOUGH I'D HALFWAY EXPECTED TO SEE ALEX there, the sudden presence of his face shocked my breath still and made me wonder if anyone else could see him.

I pushed myself up to my feet quickly and awkwardly, prioritizing getting my legs under me to maintaining any of my dignity, under the smiling observation of a trio of faces semicircled above me in a way that tickled the back of my brain and sent it searching for the resonant connection that was not forthcoming in my memory, finally getting up and pushing my hair back from my face while Alex said he was glad to see me feeling athletic after that party, that he was worried it might have all been too much for me, and I tried a sideways smile, not looking at him, and then there was another flash:

I am stumbling through the party house again, using the walls to navigate toward where I imagine the door may be, but I'm stepping around things on the floor. I can't see them because I'm looking over them, past them. Perhaps I know what they are and can't look, or perhaps I just can't look down and maintain forward momentum. Perhaps both. My foot brushes one and it gives and I recoil and I think I must know what's going on below my line of sight. There's a moaning this time, but I feel myself ignoring it...

My feet finally found the ground and I looked up at my friends, dimly aware of my skin squishing on the concrete. Alex cocked his head like he was expecting an answer so I made a little production of trying to clear water from my ear canal.

"I was saying you never really struck me as a pool-party person."

I tugged at my wet shirt, trying and failing to get it to hang right. "Well, I keep learning new things about myself this year. Self-improvement, maybe."

"Well, that's important," Trevor said.

"You don't need to improve, sugar," Megan said, in the southern accent she'd cop to fuck with you, with a look to my tangled shirt. "You're fine just how you are."

"I've seen finer," Trevor said.

But Alex didn't say anything and I tugged at my shirt some more and then struck an Olympian pose. Megan and Trevor did a little golf clap and I headed inside to look for one of those banana drinks or something else cold and boozy and tall, and found

Candace in a semicircle of people around the kitchen island, doing some stuff with fruit and rum and vodka and a blender. The blender explained some things about everybody's behavior, loose enough already that the evening was surely going to end on some weird feelings, but everyone followed Candace's lead when she turned to me and recoiled a little and made a throat noise and suddenly I was facing down a gawking jury all staring at my feet.

I followed their eyes as Candace screamed something about what the hell was I tracking into the house. The answer appeared to be some kind of blue-black goop. I wiggled my toes a bit and turned quick, holding my hands up in apology and taking as much of it as I could out the door with me before anyone could notice what I saw clear as day: the goop wasn't on my feet but seeping out of them.

Nobody outside had heard, or at least not reacted, so I shuffled around the pool deck to the door in the screen, out to the little strip of grass running between the screen and the wood fence. The grass felt obscene on the cuts on my feet, as though small squids were exploring my damaged skin. I clenched my teeth and wiped my feet on it until the feeling of something tickling the inside of my body made me queasy and then cringed back over to the screen-porch door and pressed my feet down flat on the concrete and crouched down, hoping to staunch the flow with my body weight.

Someone opened the screen door and I braced for

them to ask if I had had a bit too much or whether I needed a ride, but instead the sole of a foot pushed between my shoulder blades. I pitched forward into the grass. I rolled over and for the second time that night was looking up at Alex's grinning face.

He put out his hand and I ignored it, picking myself up onto my feet gingerly. He said that I should relax because he just couldn't resist, and why didn't I come in and have a drink.

The next thing felt foreign even as it was happening. This guy, guys of this type, I would usually just avoid until he went away, say the bare minimum to avoid it turning into some confrontation, the eruption of swaggering macho ego into pissing-match shitshow. It wasn't exactly something I felt good about, but it usually worked. It made me a little a sick but got me past the angry drunks looking for blood.

The look Alex was giving me wasn't one I hadn't seen before—like was confident he had my measure, knew what I would and wouldn't do—but suddenly there was nothing I wanted to do as much as prove him wrong.

I was bigger than him but I didn't let that phase me, so I swung at him just as hard as I could, but I didn't get the gush of blood at the stunned victim I'd hoped for. He moved his head so my knuckles didn't quite miss but caught him in the temple and I felt the crunch clear up to my elbow. He stumbled maybe two steps back but when I came back at him, trying for a spear sort of football tackle, he was back on steady feet and got his hands down around my ribs and spun, and the screen door hadn't quite closed, so we both sprawled out on the pool deck. I took a tumble, landing hard on my shoulder.

By the time I scrambled to my feet he was already bearing down, slinging his fist up from below and into my gut and all the breath rushed out of me and my arms jerked up all on their own. One of them found stubbly hair and gripped it right as my center of gravity worked its way out over the water. His head wrenched at enough of an angle that he spilled in just a second after me to a dull burst of muffled reactions from above the water. I pushed off the floor and swam toward the surface until a hand grabbed my ankle and pulled hard, so my lungs got ready for air and then had none forthcoming. He could have killed me right then but instead he dolphin-kicked up toward me and caught me under the arms and when we broke the surface my shoulders slammed against the corner of the deck.

Candace shouted something about how we boys needed to knock it off. Something floated around us in the water. And my feet throbbed without pain.

Alex held me against the edge of the pool deck, waiting for me to give up, to let him have the moment with a self-effacing laugh, but even the thought of it made my blood start to turn and seethe beyond normal limits, right into the territory of near-physical compulsion, and instead of pushing off the wall or trying to, turning the whole scene into a floating strength test I was really not convinced that I could win, I struck at the soft parts. My fingers missed his eyes but the thumb of the other hand pushed into his throat and his whole body spasmed and he took his hands off me to clutch at his neck. I dropped off the deck and smacked the back of my head against the concrete and sank back into the water.

Hands broke the surface, trailing bubbles, then whole people, and everybody worked together to haul the dazed two of us out of the pool. Alex got the steps and I got lifted and hauled over the edge to collapse not six feet from where I had sprawled before. The evening was quickly becoming a loop, with more blood on each iteration.

The reverberating pain from the crack to my head came on late and distant, like it was playing back on an old warped cassette, and I flinched into a ball and put my hands to a new sticky patch at the back of my head where the bone itself had become worryingly pliable. I suspected this wasn't just the result of a contusion but there was no time to consider it. For the moment, it was enough that the bone didn't have any holes in it.

Megan was shouting something at me when I got up but I had water in my ears, for real this time. She thought I was joking again and fixed me with a deadly look and I dug my fingers into my ears, trying to make a vacuum, until something popped wetly and I could hear everyone around me yelling.

"Dusty, are you good?" said Trevor.

And: "Dude, what the fuck is going on with you?" from Megan.

And Candace from across the pool shouting something at Alex in a register that carried its tone to me even if I couldn't make out the words, then looking over to me with steel in her eyes. She hauled Alex up by one arm, which he hung off like a maritime rescue, and walked around the deck to me, shouting that I needed to get the fuck out of her house.

Megan knew her better than I did, so she and Trevor tried interceding on my behalf, but Candace had made up her mind about what she'd seen, and sure enough it lined up with how she knew Alex better than me, had seen him around more and at gatherings where there wasn't any blood, and so the die was cast, and I saw him peeking around her shoulder, still plenty unsteady and breathing heavy, but grinning thorough the blood clinging between his teeth, pleased with his place in the world. I thought about it and decided that the rules of such things, the apologies and the long climb back into Candace's good graces, didn't really feel all that important to me right then, and with a feeling like fluorescent lights burning to the back of my eye sockets, I lunged.

Candace got her hands on one of my shoulders and got me turned halfway around, but I corrected on the way enough to bash my palms into Alex's face. The impact I expected didn't come for a second, though, and not until after my fingers' skin stuck against his, like pulp in a cheesecloth, but the bones slipped through, and then my wrists hit bone and bounced back, leaving bright red divots in his face that held their shape for a moment before popping out and restoring his face to its normal shape and gushing bright red down the side of it. He stumbled back, clutching at his cheekbones in a way that made my skin tingle. Eyes wide, as unsure of what had happened as I was but feeling very differently about it, eyes and mouth and fingers stretching wide until Candace broke my concentration on him, on what he was going to do next, and I spun to her and my skin gave as easily as before, expect when I pulled my hand back my skin stopped being so malleable while my bones were still splayed inside her skin, and she coughed hard, spraying bile and blood all over my chest, and carried me with her flailing momentum back into Alex and we all three sprawled toward the pool but crashed down before it in slick spray across the concrete.

Megan and Trevor made a mistake: they ran up to help us. Megan got her hands under my arms and Trevor grabbed Alex, and the bones in my hand turned to jelly just long enough for them to slip out of Candace's skin and back into my own. It caused some kind of itch and as Megan hauled me up to my feet I spun on her and tried to grind it out against her face, jolting her back, and when she'd recovered she jerked back again and clawed at her face like trying to scrape something off, and Trevor came at me, catching me in the lower back and I just went limp to go with the force of the blow but he couldn't get a grip so he slipped past me and landed hard.

And then Megan came up with some bear spray from her bag, and Trevor pulled a pocketknife from his boot and crawled up to his feet. Those who hadn't paid attention up to now sure fucking started, and I found myself with a pool deck full of eyes pinning me down like a caught butterfly, and thinking back about how I ended up here but it had happened so fast, and now I had my only friends in the whole wide party brandishing weapons at me, and so I turned and ran out the same screen door Alex and I had crashed in through, around the lawn and out the wood fence and a block down the street before I remembered I'd driven—driven and parked—and so I circled back and there was no one swarming my truck, no one waiting for me, but that wouldn't hold long. They were surely still tending to the wounded, so I hurried to get in the truck and drive, only to pull over a mile or less from the house, before the main road and within the brick-façade barriers of the subdivision, shove the door open, and sprawl my way roadward spraying thin bile out onto the asphalt, and the arm of the hand I gripped around the oh-shit handle to steady myself held for a bit, while I was gasping and spitting my mouth clean, and then it gave, and not where there was a joint. The bone didn't snap but bent, and I lurched forward and gasped against the pain that was surely coming. Instead, I felt something localized and confusing, a pointed tingling that made me want to squirm not to get away from it, but rather to better feel the strangely pleasant sensation, like a muscle relaxing out of a stress position. The bone snapped back straight and I hauled myself back into the cab, and relaxed a second, waiting for the sense-memory to pass, and then my skin was tight all over, like it was getting vacuum-sealed to my bones.

I scrambled in the passenger seat, through the plastic bags full of wrappers and empty bottles from my most recent workday until I found a half-full liter of water and poured it down my throat. It swept out a heavy layer of dust, all the way down to my stomach and out through my muscle, and there was a gleaming pocket of clarity under all of it, the clammy shaking of the last few days giving way to a cool calm for a couple heartbeats, in which I got a look at my situa-tion as though from a comfortable distance, at the state of my face and my truck and the friendships bleeding out back at the house, and what I remember of that little glimpse was a strong sense of teetering, the kind of precariousness you can see clear as day from just a few paces away, and honestly I'd known I was in bad shape but just then it was like I'd stepped out of time and caught a look at it before the constric-tion set in again, the brief flood sucked back to punishing tightness and I licked my lips to no partic-ular avail and drove home in such a jerky manner it's a minor miracle I didn't hit a traffic stop or something more solid, and put my head under the faucet in the sink.

I gulped until my neck strained from the angle I was holding it at and then reared up gasping. The water helped a bit but I was soon thirsty again, so I stripped off and got down on my belly in the bathtub and yanked the knob. It blasted painfully cold on my back, which started turning toward the painfully hot before I got my hand up and popped the faucet depressor down, and I pulled the temperature knob and didn't quite wait until the water got cold again to start slurping. However much I may have burned my lips and tongue, the flood of cold water brought me all the way around, over and over. Every time I filled up the old stomach and depleted the lungs, I pulled my face up from the stream and gasped down some air until thirsty replaced drowning and I dipped my mouth down again. Every time I came up there were new changes happening in my body, tissues slipping and squishing, but I couldn't feel them when I drank, so I sucked down as much water as I could.

– – – – –

I woke up with my face in a little pool of water around the drain, aware that my tongue flicking out to grab at the water was what did it. The notion made my stomach turn, imagining myself scrounging off the bathtub I knew exactly how long it had been since I really cleaned, and I struggled not to puke all the water back up.

Wandering around my place proved no more or less useful or enlightening than the similar attempt I'd made recently around Mike's. It was all just my apartment, my stuff, my residue. I still hadn't tracked Mike down and he was maybe the only friend I had left, and certainly the only one I expected to understand my situation even as far as I did.

But my skin was already tingling, and even a night in the trickling bathtub only left such relief as found itself drying off me after a few minutes up and about.

I finally started putting the two together and went back to the bathroom and got the water going but didn't want to peel my old clothes off the floor, so I went to the plastic bin I'd been using for a dresser, next to the one I'd been using for a hamper, doing a quick sniff test to make sure I'd gotten the right one, and brought one day's worth to the bathroom. I thought about just doing a tee shirt and boxers in order to keep myself light, mobile, but light meant less water and so I stuck everything I had under the stream and squished my fingers around and then worked my way through three layers of sodden cotton, more by far than I would have worn for the weather, then went back for a hoodie and soaked that too. I tried to find my boots but remembered kicking them off at Candace's, so I squished my wet socks into a pair of sneakers and made my dripping way to my truck and sat down and felt a pool gathering, squeezing out from the fabric clinging to me and dripping off my body, and felt pretty steady.

I headed over to Mike's place and circled the complex looking for anything that stood out, anything to keep me from trying the apartment again. I wasn't sure what day it was by this point, but the sun was up and most of the cars were gone so I figured it was a workday. That didn't explain why Mike's car wasn't in his space, I didn't think, but that didn't stop me from parking in it and walking right up to the door and finding it unlocked.

Did I leave it unlocked when I left? I decided that

I certainly had and stepped through, and then convinced myself that I hadn't, but no one leapt out to make me pay for if I was wrong; it was just the same place I'd been however many days ago, the kind of neat you keep up when you live alone and don't have people over much, a kind of distributed clutter, clean in the frequently used areas and the messiest just adjacent to them. It wasn't like I could tell whether anything had been moved but it didn't feel like it, and the place at least hadn't been ransacked, so I walked around some more, dripping on the carpet, which I only noticed after I'd paced around the apartment and stopped after looking behind the couch for the fourth time and saw a trail of deep depressions in the carpet. I looked around like there would be something ready to hand I could use to remove this trace of myself, but of course there wasn't, there's never really any way to extract oneself from the places one enters and inhabits and interacts with, and some of the footprints were already drying up, the carpet soaking up the water cast off from my body, and the thought of it made me suddenly nauseated in a much more philosophical way than I had been dealing with, so I put the shower on hot and stepped in until the warmth soaked its way through my clothes to my skin. I took the walk to the front door in as long of strides as I could manage weighted down with wet clothes like that, as though it would keep more of me from getting into the carpet, and got into my truck and drove.

Mike wasn't the sort of friend I knew where he

hung out, if he hung out at all, which seemed unlikely; he had his job and he kicked it with our mutual friends, but I'd be hard pressed to guess where else he might spend his time, a man who liked to socialize but liked his apartment just as well. I got on the highway but the elevation and the speed of traffic made the world thin, like it was going to let go of me and let me spin away and then itself dissolve, and this feeling got worse so I kept slowing down until the spinning slowed and I could see right, but then it started again, caught up with me and set in harder, so I slowed down more to try and keep ahead of it, and the traffic whipping by me grew voices and somehow I'd wound up one lane from the right so I had to change and nearly took out a minivan on my way over to the exit ramp.

It let out on a road in between places. I didn't recognize any of the buildings or the street signs, but I eased around them a little at a more comfortable speed and closer to the ground and my lungs opened all the way back up. I pointed the car in about the direction the highway had been taking me.

Somewhere in the panic of the freeway an idea completed. Despite how badly I wanted to ignore it, there were at most two places I knew that Mike was likely to be holed up, if that's what he was: the people he was closest to, and who he'd turn to if he found himself in the first personal crisis I'd ever known him to have, were Trevor and Megan. I had already been driving more or less in the right direction, so I wound my way through until I got near downtown and found Megan's neighborhood of small but well-kept houses tucked between a middle school and a row of liquor stores and restaurants.

Trevor was out the front door by the time I was halfway up the walk, flying out in a controlled not-quite-run to grab me by the shirt and drag me into the house, like that wasn't where I was already headed. He clipped my ribs against the closing screen door on the way and my vision blurred and I was pretty sure there was new dampness there, underneath the soaking clothes. The carpet came up fast and smacked me in the cheek. Before I could blink myself clear, Trevor jerked my collar up toward him and blasted the bridge of my nose. Hot blood ran down the back of my throat and out my mouth in a couple of sharp coughs, misting Trevor's face, and he hit me again, and the strange itching sponginess I was feeling at Candace's surged through my skin but it seemed as hampered by the probable concussion as I was, so it was just a few crawling roiling patches. Trevor went to continue caving in my face but Megan stepped over and caught him by the elbow.

I tried to say, "All my friends are here," but I think my mouth was too gummed up with blood to make much sense.

"You notice his clothes are all wet, too?" Megan said.

"Who gives a shit?"

"Are you fucking serious?"

I opened my mouth to make up a story but blood started dripping down my throat again, so I rolled over and coughed my way through their conference. I got back on my back and there the two of them were, looking down at me again like they had poolside, but this time Trevor reached down and hauled me up by my shirt and my neck, having altogether less trouble than I would have expected, and dragged me to the bathroom and tossed me in, so I landed on the damp rug in front of the sink and rolled from it to the bathmat next to the tub, and it was damp too, and the tile was damp. The whole bathroom was damp and Megan said from the doorway that they knew it was me even if they didn't know how or why but Trevor had some different ideas about how the conversation was going to go, or else it was just bad-cop time, and he pitched me into the tub.

My hand went in first. A feeling like a water balloon, then like jello-firm surface tension, then a jiggling mass splitting under pressure. A warm and not entirely unpleasant stench poofing out, like something sweet only just starting to turn. The jelly pressing hard into itself, trying to hold onto my hand until I pulled it out.

I fell back on the bathmat and saw Trevor upside-down coming at me and I worked at getting upright before he hit me again, and then I could see directly into the tub, the tepid water around what may once

-----

have been skin but was filled to stretching in tub-length bubble, and Mike's face twisted into an oblivious mask.

It didn't look like skin, mostly, was too transparent, enough that I could see the veins in their two-color rainbow showing as though through a Vaseline balloon, and then I was choking down vomit, and then he moved, then Mike fucking moved, and I saw every piece of underlying contraction, every muscle squishing into itself and how it impacted each of the blood vessels around it, and I saw Mike's face move forward on top of that and look at me.

Trevor grabbed me again by the divots in my shirt still shaped like his fingers. "You did this too, right? You did something to Candace, man, we've seen her, and then you did something worse to Mike."

The timeline didn't work out at all, no way did what happened to Mike start after I had my interaction with Candace, but all I could manage was, "Before?" and all that got me was slammed back against the tub hard enough that it took me a few moments to realize the knocking I heard was Megan's knuckles on the doorframe, not something in my head. It took a while for the sound to mean anything to Trevor, too.

"His clothes are fucking *wet*, Trevor."

Trevor held me down by the shoulder and patted me down, like they hadn't already talked about this, felt my shirt and tee shirt and jeans and sweater all soaked through, and not just damp on the top layers from some rain we didn't have today, and then sat back on his heels with his hand gripping my collar and looking at me like it was time to decide what part to cut off.

Megan suggested it might be a good time to start talking, so I tried, starting with the ex that I was pretty sure wasn't ex and then waking up and how my body had been fucking up since. How my skin was different, but I tried to leave out how it seemed like I was changing, and I guess they keyed into the absence.

Their general position, expressed with degrees of profanity and threats of physical violence, was that I had best explain what had happened to Mike. I could see their point, and tried to tell them that's what I wanted to find out, too, but Trevor cracked me on the head, and suddenly:

I'm in the living room, recoiling off the wall and I can't find my way to the door. The carpet hums up through my boots and the air conditioner has that ball-in-a-tube rattle to its whine, and up through that I start to hear a round sound like the groan that follows a concussion or someone losing their last bit of patience, but constant, with just little bumps in it giving it something like rhythm. I finally get up the nerve to look down...

And Megan was coming in with a knife I never knew her to carry, shouting about talk, motherfucker, and so I talked some more, about being constantly thirsty and my skin changing from time to time and these flashes of maybe-memory coming through the

-----

haze more and more. I took a breath finally, and when I had air for more words, I told them how I went to the shindig at Candace's looking for Mike in the first place, that I thought maybe he'd been going through the same things I had after the party.

"And what, nobody at that house is having this?"

I told her I hadn't known anybody else at that party. We all, for the first time since I got there, sat in silence for a few seconds, listening to how that sounded. To me, it sounded a lot like a breaking point, so I said how Alex was the source of the fucked-up drugs.

Trevor actually turned away from me, throwing his hands up. "For fuck sake, he doesn't deal, man. Jesus, if you'd taken him up on that job, you'd know he doesn't have to."

"Maybe he does it for fun, then. Maybe it was just to fuck with me and Mike. You really trust that guy?"

We could have gone a couple more rounds, made sure we'd exhausted all of each other's objections, but instead what was always going to happen happened right away.

Trevor spat about how he should have listened to our guy's warnings about me and shoved me back against the tub, elbows and hands keeping all the rele-vant parts of my head and arms pressed against the porcelain. He wasn't attacking me but pinning me down, like pre-surgery, like mounting a butterfly.

Megan crouched in front of me, holding her knife out in front of her with both hands. "Maybe something's happening to you, sure. Yeah. I saw the fight. I felt how your hand was when you took a swing at me. But you still look like you, and well. You can see why I don't think something happened to the two of you together. I think you did this."

"I think," I said, licking my lips and trying for maybe the very last time to appear calm, in control, "that you are about to make a very big mistake."

Megan shrugged, said at least I seemed to know where this was going, and put the knife up at the level of my face and moved it slow toward my throat and turned at the last second for my ear and so I rolled that way and grabbed at her clothes and heaved her into the tub.

She squished to a stop in whatever made up Mike now and kicked and flailed a couple times until her rational mind kicked in and reminded her just what she was clawing new grooves into and lay mostly still, turning her head to the side to breathe through where her shoulder had just gouged Mike. Trevor popped to his feet but he didn't move toward the door, just stood there watching.

It held for a few seconds until Mike finally reacted.

First, the skin-jelly closed over Megan's arm up to her shoulder. She screamed briefly and the enclosure continued, sucking up her neck and over her head. Her one free hand slapped impotently against the surface. I tried to look for a way to get her free but Trevor shoved me to the side and reached behind the toilet tank and pulled out a gun.

He squeezed two rounds off into Mike, knocking himself back a step and all my senses into porcelain echo. When I got my eyes back open there were two divots in Mike's skin. I could see the bullets suspended in the jelly, and Trevor could too, but before he could fire again two jets of flesh burst out from the new holes and slapped against his chest and his gut, dimpling the skin down hard like they were going to impale him, thick dishwater spears, but once his clothes gave way the tendrils softened all along their length, relaxing from hard beams into loopy jiggling curls, and something started happening under Trevor's shirt, a squirming and bulging, tendrils and skin both. I tried to picture how they were coming together, knitting themselves into each other. It was at best an incomplete picture, but vivid enough I imagined an amped-up version of what happened to Alex's face, to Candace's chest, and Trevor's mouth opened and then stretched wider and wider, like he was getting ready to try and swallow something. And then the opposite happened.

A bundle of tight white tubes wriggled their way out of his mouth and stretched away from each other, like the larger ones that cut into him had divided into dozens and stretched themselves lighter. Megan surely couldn't see or hear what was going on but she started to kick anyway. I heard a quick squelching and then the kicking stopped for a second and then frantically started up again. A muffled crack brought on an even more distant scream and she went still.

The tendrils coming out of Trevor jerked further apart and whipped around and then it was like they figured out how to be fingers and grabbed the molding and the tub and the sink and pulled all at once and Trevor's eyes bulged until the rending of his mouth pushed the skin up over them and the ripping from deep in his torso dimmed them forever. The tentacles gripped harder and Trevor's insides came out, splashing on the bathroom floor and filling the space with a vile meat stink. A rush of blood and bile splashed out before the heavy thunk of his stomach pulling itself inside out and through his teeth and out in a dripping pouch to the floor.

Trevor finally toppled over and I received the splash and spatter of his innards on my face and clothes with something less than the appropriate level of concern, which itself worried me; on a visceral level, what was happening around me on linoleum and porcelain and big-box-store bathware felt perfectly natural, like whatever I was becoming was fine with all this.

I looked over into the tub and saw Megan's face, twisted around and staring at me as though through a dirty snow globe. Our eyes met as the cuts in my feet reopened at the touch of Trevor's gore and seeped out some of my own and I started to see things, like the visions I had been having but without the benefit of lines and borders, so they were flashes of light that I sensed a memory lurking underneath but could not access. Megan's mouth may have opened in something like shock, or I may have misinterpreted an effect of her floating.

The blood was foreign on my open feet but not unpleasantly, not like the grass in Candace's lawn, and as the flashes of visions slowly faded, I started to feel what it was like in that moment for Megan, and it was nothing all that pleasant, and what it was like for Trevor, and it was a quickly dimming light, but what I felt from Mike was shockingly expansive, like he was taking in this scene and a half-dozen others and all of the scenes from his life that these feelings called up. It was an incomprehensible rush that I couldn't do anything about, or move or think, until they passed, like they filled all the spare synapses in my brain. When I came back to the immediate world, the floor was covered with wriggling gray worms, dotted and speckled all over with torn remnants of Trevor's stomach, a gory wriggling carpet.

Crumpled in the corner where the wall met the floor, held partly up by the hardware-store molding with its landlord-special white paint already flaking off to reveal the dirtier white underneath, the rest of Trevor slumped, drained, only looking full around the mouth where the bouquet of tendrils erupted. They had mostly settled their thrashing for the moment, had settled into twisting among themselves on the bathroom floor, more precise movements that nonetheless required the occasional tug on the source to gain a little more slack, and at those moments, not much further apart than a heartbeat, his body twitched all over. The slack the jerking afforded let the strands fold over and under each other, knotting themselves together and greasing each other with the particles of Trevor they ground finer and finer between them. The bloody weave tightened and filled in the gaps in itself until it pushed itself up against the sides of my feet, until there was nowhere for them to go but the wounds from under the floor of Candace's swimming pool.

I saw myself in a rush from three angles all at once, laid atop my own vision, which grew watery and indistinct. I saw myself from below, from the skewed vantage of Trevor's dangling head; from the inside of the bloated Mike-thing in the tub, from which Megan stared; from an impossibly stretched vantage, the corner of the room curving around my pale damp trembling ass. I tried to move, less a belated urge to flee than to find a place to stand that wasn't covered in a burst piece of Trevor, but it was impossible to orient with just one of the four images I was seeing at the same time, so I went nowhere, sent my feet in different directions and pitched forward, hitting my shoulder on the edge of the towel rack and then my forehead against the wall, but the tendrils in my foot rushed deeper and clenched and kept me from falling. They pushed up into my legs, ignoring the regular pathways of veins and fluids but carving a pattern of their own. I was pinned against the wall and saw myself writhe through three sets of eyes though I had no sensation of doing so, and suddenly the tremors

-----

stopped cold and what I felt was increased movements, deeper under the skin than the six eyes could
see, and I slumped down into a soft and slimy sea of
alien flesh.

I arrived at the floor a ready vessel.

– – – –

THE TENDRILS IN MY LEGS STIFFENED AND I FOUND that they had worked their way further north than I had expected. My lower back twinged and cramped and a syrupy numbness radiated out until it reached just below my neck. I lay out of view of my new vision, with the exception of a glimpse of my foot through Trevor. The tendrils worked to create new angles of entry in addition to the ones I came equipped with, into which—eyes, nostrils, ass—they were already prying and pushing. My skin gave way in a wholly unnatural and frankly pleasurable way, tearing itself gamely open in a fashion I didn't need to see to understand, and a prick of a tingling jolted, cool and crackling, up my spine and along my teeth and out through a clutch of new limp limbs sprouting out the top of my skull. I felt it course out and into the diffuse mass of Mike and Megan's rapidly dimming nerves. Mike had spilled well into the tub's drainpipe, and I felt every friction between the oozing flesh and the copper, every strand of the moldering hair clinging together into the beginnings of a clog along the bottom of the first turn in the pipe. I felt all the sensations of the bodies I was now connected to by blood and muscle, whether that individual node in our viscous network was itself alive in the usual sense.

The sense of bodily individuality does not long outlive the evidence of the senses, and so my brain clicked over a few times, like cycling through frequencies until it found one that fit, and already the sense of my physical self was more expansive. I reached out my arm but instead a chunk of Mike flexed and sprang back. I tried again and moved a section of the tendrils bursting from Trevor. It took me several minutes to get the hang of wriggling my body, my first body, along my tentacles toward the tub, a couple more to hoist myself up into the too-warm flesh of my new swollen bathtub body. I worried briefly about air but I felt no burning in my lungs, even as long seconds passed and I took none in. Oxygen came in through some other mechanism, and rather than ponder the effect I plunged deeper, shoving my face through the firm jelly of what used to be Mike, and the further I pushed the more energized I felt, and I reached the bottom of the tub and crawled forward toward the drain, dragging Trevor's tendrils and streaks of Megan's blood through Mike. I did it like I was swimming through a pool, doing the crawl, and each stroke took me less far than I expected it to and swirled the pieces of my once-friends around my limbs, mingling with each other and then seeping into me. I pulled the gel toward myself and a thin layer of my skin flecked wetly off and dissolved; I pulled again and the matter began to merge with my outer flesh. My arms stretched out of shape. Bones distorted and warped, but without a crack or a splinter, and their deformations pushed outward until they became like noodles. It didn't seem like there was enough room in the tub for this transformation to happen, but it happened anyway, so when I got to the drain, with Mike's skin stretching and forming a sort of shell for me, I found my skull had likewise elongated, and it followed my hands and my arms down through the open hole.

My entrance squeezed and squished more loudly than I expected, in stark contrast to the numb, muted silence that had overtaken the bathroom. I got deep enough in that my new body should have been free of drag from the outside, but something caught. I pushed harder and stretched a little until, though the harder parts of my body freely bent now, if with a bit more resistance than the surrounding tissue, they reached a point at which they didn't quite hurt but did send an alarm.

I had been focusing, I realized, on my front and sides, so I relaxed and did whatever my new equivalent of taking a breath was and reached back, along the S-bend and out the drain and over the lip of the tub and found the tendrils I had used to push myself up into the tub in the first place, and before too long I wound my way through to the fattest part of the loop, where they divided and fell back into the Trevor part of me, and out into the tips of the ones still flopping free. They had pulled each other away from being an even coating on the floor into clumps with strands between.

At first it was impossible to move them. I tried to pull a strand and it moved a little bit but just got pulled tighter in the tangle. I stopped pulling before it got too much worse and thought about swimming underwater, like if you'd just dove in, and how you wouldn't think about each leg then, but about your whole body from the waist down as a rolling unit making a sort of wave underwater, and I tried for something like that. My tentacles hopped a few times in no particular direction and then I got a better roll going and I steered them toward the tub. The first to get there flapped about half the way up the side, but stuck loosely to the surface and slid very slowly down, giving me enough time to roll again and flip them further up. I got the leading edge in, then a little more, and eventually gravity started to work with me instead of against me. As soon as the first hardened muscle-fluid splashed into the water, the tendrils squirted out from their tangle and slithered toward the drain on their own.

The rest of the tentacles plopped into the tub, cutting into the now-stretched Mike and splashing the remnants of the water. Some of them sank into my

----

growing accumulation of flesh while others wriggled along the porcelain, getting grip with their tips and leverage with the elbows, rushing to join the rest of my mass down the pipe.

Pressing forward into the pipe felt a little unsteady, a little deer-learning-to-run, but it was smoother than feet on concrete—it had a little glide to it that kept my stumbles to a minor crumpling somewhere along my body, not a real break in forward motion. The pressure from the walls of the pipe worked with some slime the Mike-jelly gave off in response to keep me moving steadily, even when I had to pause momentarily to reorient some part of my body. I dove deeper and deeper into the shockingly intricate network of pipes underneath the town, like a mirror suburb of copper and steel and concrete, tracing the seams and gaps of the aboveground one, the parts that make things work and so must be kept hidden. At first it was a dizzying labyrinth, but the more I pushed through, the more the bends were stored in a growing muscle-memory map. The sense of discovery made for a powerful motivator. I rushed through as much as I could, squeezing through corners I didn't know for sure I could make and bursting into the larger main lines, building a mental picture of my hometown that was more three-dimensional than I expected, that made me wonder how many specialized tradespeople and bureaucrats would have to be gathered in the same office, and for how long, to put together as clear a blueprint of our total sprawl as I was gathering. I pushed a little further, a little faster, and felt more and more like I was making a new discovery within the layers of subterranean footprint corresponding to each year's new construction.

That, until I finally pushed down a few dozen years too far and found myself a little more stuck than I had been before and came to a real stop, and the narrow pipes that had encouraged my passage suddenly shrank to a terrifying compression. The walls had been touching my sides as they bombed by but now it was a static pressure, and I wiggled from side to side to see if it would dislodge my back end any quicker, but all it did was drive home how limited my range of motion was and I felt panic rising up, kicking through me like humming power lines, and my vision narrowed and the pipe clutching me started to feel soft and pulsing and then:

I'm bouncing off the wall and kicking my foot against something soft, and finally looking down at the living room floor and I see ten or twelve fucked-up kids kneeling in a circle. The buzz from the speaker system isn't all that loud but it's dialed in to come up through the carpet and out from the middle of my bones. The people in the circle bob along to the pulse. Each of them has their right hand pressed palm-down on the floor. The one I bumped into flinches away, but the one next to them reaches out and grabs my leg when I try to stumble past and I pitch and overcorrect and fall on my face in the middle of the circle, and catch, just for a second out of the corner of my eye, a man in a black tee shirt and faded jeans…

I came back to myself when my body finally wriggled free and started moving forward, like my muscles remembered what I had been up to while I was gone. My motion squelched a little louder than it had before, and as I kept peeling around the joints and junctions another sound emerged from underneath that one, an insistent low rumble. I was suddenly more focused on finding a way out or at least a firm point of orientation than mapping for the thrill of it, so I didn't notice these new sounds until they had been coming for a while. I was aware when I heard them that I had been hearing them for some time. They sounded familiar, like voices I'd heard before stripped of all their internal echo, made flat and deep. They were coming from inside my body, and I wasn't clear enough about which was which to tell them apart, but one of them picked up on something that was said back in Megan's house or just knew what I wanted or was about to want and talked about where Alex was living.

He had secured a PO box years ago, just in case, and kept the precaution of having all his mail sent there and dealing with it a couple times a week. It was a neat enough move for tricking lazy cops and keeping whatever he was receiving through the post from prying eyes and sticky fingers, but I was neither the law nor the mail and I had a clear sense of direc-

tion from my new advisors and a less expected angle
of approach.

– – –

I PUSHED THROUGH THE SEWER UNTIL I BURST OUT
into a larger pipe and then up a narrower one that
broke into individual lines. It all said apartment
complex. I wriggled my way up and waited for my
mental map to fit together with the one I was
receiving from inside my body, moving around in
roughly a circle to make sure I didn't get stuck and
take another trip to that fucked-up afterparty, and
soon enough I was oozing my way toward one drain
in particular. This drain cover was the kind with
several pinholes poked into a solid cap, a little trap to
keep hair out of the pipe that was threatening to keep
me out of the tub. I braced myself and started to ease
on through, splitting myself into greasy spaghetti and
a ragged bathroom, all rusty red bathtub corners and
mildewing caulk. I pushed the tenacles out ahead of
my splitting body and rode up them to the lip of
another tub and over onto tile-patterned linoleum in

an empty bathroom with an open door. My body, readjusting in its new gooey way to the sausage-grinder manner of my entrance, bounced out from the compression and the stretching and started to glom back together when an unfamiliar man in his boxer shorts filled the doorway, scratching himself in a no-one's-looking sort of way.

He froze there with a couple fingers curled around his balls and opened his mouth to scream and before I'd fully thought about it I threw a grip of tentacles at his face. His mouth and his eyes were covered right away and the tips of two strands turned around his earlobes, squeezing as they went, but all of a sudden they all pulled back, releasing and hovering an inch off the guy's skin and a real-life scream rose to meet the one Trevor started in my head, saying a name and instructions I couldn't quite make out, so I pushed through his resistance and clamped back down. The new pressure was less controlled and the man's skull came to pieces like glassware, brains and bone catching in my limbs like a strainer, blood pattering out onto the linoleum, until there wasn't enough head left to keep a grip on and the body splashed to the floor.

The man's gore felt terrible on my skin, like a turning stomach but on the outside. I pulled back, still not entirely having mastered moving around but getting at least pretty competent at bathrooms. I was trying to get myself steady to head out into the rest of house, but Alex must have heard something because he appeared in the doorway where his roommate had been and I don't know what he made of me in that moment, but he clocked the blood and the body and moved fast, taking a quick step back and slamming the door. Echoes of Trevor screamed at me from deep in my body, though I couldn't say if he was insisting on a course of action or demanding that I stop or reacting to his transformation and new situation, focusing as I was all my attention forward. I wasn't sure if I could manage the doorknob and I didn't want to spend the time trying to squeeze under the door, so I gathered myself and pushed my back end against the side of the bathtub and slammed into the middle of the door as hard as I could. The wood cracked down the middle and the hinges bent. I shoved forward one more time and the crack bowed outward and the top hinge gave way and I had a V-shaped opening to burst through and spill onto short rough carpet. The coarse thickness stuck and pulled at parts of my body, and they strung behind me like discarded chewing gum while I crashed toward the front door, which Alex had dropped the pants he was pulling up halfway down his thighs to yank the handle of. He disappeared into the blinding sunshine and I barreled over, tentacles leading the way. The light touched my body and washed through it, lighting everything up and blasting away my ability to perceive the difference between things, leaving not a solid white screen but a dry smearing, and I whipped my feelers as widely as I could for as long as I could stand

it, until I had to pull myself back into the dark apartment and found, to my surprise in my returning sight,
Alex dragged in after me, clear strands wrapped
around his lower legs and winding their way up, blood
streaming from concrete burns on his forehead and
his hands.

He came up swinging but couldn't quite figure out
where my weak spots were. We had that in common.
He landed a couple wet blows, like slapping water
with his fists, and my feelers tightened just a little and
he forgot everything else and screamed like his femur
was on the verge of snapping.

I brought him close and tried to speak but didn't
produce anything by those efforts except a little
gurgling, a shifting of my interior. I tried to talk to
him directly, like Megan and Trevor had been
talking at me, but of course that didn't work.
Finding this apartment had been fueled by fury and
bloodlust, but now that I was there I remembered
that what I wanted in the first place—after a cure,
recovery, which was clearly no longer an option—
was answers, and the growing impression that even
with a newly captive audience I couldn't get that
made me want to scream, to find a way to scream
and then do it, and I clenched and heaved until my
face—my old face, my original face—pushed
forward to the edge of my new body enough for my
captive to recognize it, and while he reacted with the
open mouth and wide eyes of a man recognizing at
last a way out from his suffering, I began to hear my

own voice, muted and gummy but recognizably mine.

"What? What?" he said, and though I couldn't sense whether he was reacting to the situation or failing to make out my words, I repeated myself:

"What did you do to me?"

"What?"

And that was about the end of my admittedly strained patience. His femurs didn't give, not with the little bit that I increased my pressure, but I could tell they hurt plenty, and I imagined his toes turning purple, his feet starting to swell.

"There were a bunch of people in a circle. On the living-room floor. After you had me sell those drugs. After you drugged me."

"What, that wiccan shit? Fuck, fuck, I don't know. And I what? You think that I've got so much shit that I'm going to slip you some just to fucking—I don't know, to fuck with you? Why would I do that?"

"If you wanted me for something. You did this to me, and you're going to tell me what it is."

He called me some names and screamed and thrashed against his bonds and then screamed hoarser, and I reared my remaining tentacles up and drove their tips into his chest, thinking to talk to him in a more direct way, one in which he was not so practiced at lying. None of my new internal voices thought that this was a good idea, but soon I couldn't hear them anymore. My new interface brought in new panicked screaming, loud to start and getting louder, but without the physical limitations of the physical throat, so it didn't distort as it grew, like the volume was a gel or a balloon expanding to fill all the spaces in my skull until not only my companions but my very own thoughts were flushed away. I forced my way through it to scream something of my own, the memories I had of the end of the party and the flashes I'd been having which may well have been the same thing, and I felt a little bit of a response from Alex about it, recognition but with something else behind it, something that it took me a beat to recognize as doubt, like what he was seeing wasn't exactly how he remembered it. I was thinking about how to get more specific about the discrepancy when something started in his brain. I pulled back, waiting for him to come back around, and when that didn't work I pushed forward, shouting harder into him as deep as I could, but this to sparked no response. I ran the same routine a few more times, pulling back and then shoving back in, until his mind started to grow stale, the way a house left untended for long enough starts to feel different in ways beyond the obvious, like the air tastes wrong, and I had to accept that I had gotten all that I was going to get.

I yanked my tentacles out in frustrated disgust and the body launched to the couch and slammed against the bottom of it. If Alex was still in there, he didn't make any move to cushion himself.

In the silence that followed, before Megan and Trevor and Mike's voices set in again, I started to feel

---

like I knew what was happening to me, what had happened to me, and the drug was involved but only as a part of something else, something larger and more elusive. It was like some kind of constraint had been lifted, a plastic vacuum pack around my flesh breaking and my body only now beginning to get past the springing-out phase and into the settling-into-its-shape point. I had no idea yet what form I might be jiggling into but I felt that something inside of me hadn't formed yet or had consumed itself, a strange hollowness despite the crowding.

Mike piped up, a guttural sort of vibration like a passing train that had gotten drowned out by all the screaming before, slurring on about all of his bones turning to mush and pulling himself around on skin that started stretching out underneath and behind him and then about some things he'd been seeing and how lost himself for days at a time in these visions, and he didn't stop or pause when I lost track of his stream and so I had to plug back in as best I could, so I wasn't tracking the whole thing but I got enough to know I was glad my story and his diverged. I had a sense it was something to do with my water maneuvers, like it changed the order of things so that if I hadn't kept it together, exactly, I did better than I might have.

Trevor shrieked at me, voice fresher and clearer, steamed that I had ruined whatever chance I thought I had of finding out what if anything really happened and trailed off into a low wail, while Megan hissed a low violence that once I keyed into it I could follow from the pieces of her inside me through to her prodding efforts to find a way to hurt me, to strike against her new situation in a too-late way that I could very much understand.

The three vibrations floated mostly close to each other until they rubbed against each other with a bone-buzzing dissonance and then back apart again, like high-tension wires blown against each other in a high wind, with no pattern but the inevitability of another clash.

All the clanging, following on the frustration of my main goal and the realization that I wasn't going to receive my answer or the accompanying hope of a cure—I want to claim that I wasn't sure what I was about to try and do, or if I was that I didn't think it could work, but neither is close to the truth. More accurately, it was with desperate hope that I started, thinking that this new crowded mind of mine, more than anything else, would break me.

So I followed Megan's lead, except working in the other direction; I clenched up the parts of me nearest where she was trying to strike, like tightening your abs for a crunch but in more directions and with the meat that makes up the mind folding along with a strange sort of tickling feeling, and squeezed all of the parts of Megan as close to the center as I could and then squeezed some more. Eventually compression became crushing and her voice cut off, sudden enough that I remembered, like a home-video flash from another life, what Megan had meant to me, and had to tell myself all about how that wasn't really Megan anymore, or soon wouldn't be, and bring myself around to focus on Trevor. The parts of him were more distinct, clustered around the ends of the tenacles he brought to the party, and took more force but less wriggling to crush. Mike was a different problem, making up the bulk of my body. I couldn't feel him moving or locate a center for his voice like the other two, and I started to grasp frantically, feeling around randomly and fast, and my sense of my own insides started to fade and I felt it starting, if only just, the drifting away of my brain from any real control of my body, so I pulled back, tried to relax. Things held as they were, and I sucked a lungful of air through my skin into the body-thing that I was becoming, and waited until I started to feel the pieces of my body, more like a gently differentiated totality than a bunch of solids in a gel, so that the remnants of Mike were streaks, harder to find but not impossible if I let things go quiet for a few moments. I stretched my long self out along the entryway and into the living room, catching a wave of molecular relief at stretching out like that, if on top of a renewed sense of vertigo in response to the sheer size of my body now, the way my brain still expected it to take up one amount of space and reality another, and starting thrusting in from the far points as sharply as I could, shifting the Mike parts of myself toward the middle in ragged streaks.

I waited until the sorting seemed to be as done as it was likely to get and rooted around for that hole I had felt inside of myself, to see if it had a physical equivalent, and shoved my three companions down as far as I could, and into each other, and there was no more screaming, just a deafening series of crunches and a sudden heaviness of my extremities, like someone turned the gravity dial way up on just those parts, so when I began scrambling back to the bathroom all the ease of movement I'd felt before was replaced by a crushing heaviness, not just that every motion took more effort than it previously had, but in the way that if you pay too close of attention to what should be broad muscle movements, like pouring from a jug into a bottle or walking down a narrow flight of stairs, it gets harder. I had to focus on movements now that had come so easily at first, and I wasn't as good at it, not at all. It seemed like the company I'd briefly had was more active than I thought and had been doing more of the lifting. It's a particular kind of terror, knowing that what you thought was your body was in fact the operation of multiple entities. The place to learn to drive a forklift isn't when there's a truck that needs unloaded, but there was nobody else left in my body to do it.

— —

THE TENTACLES DIDN'T MOVE NEAR AS SMOOTHLY AS they had, no question of getting a good glide going. I wielded them in clumsy clumps, like fists instead of fingers, until I got back to the edge of the tub. Sitting there stationary, I felt caught tight between my sluggish limbs and a gaping emptiness, where I had the suffocating sense that the limbs I'd only just begun to get used to were going to lock all the way up and leave me trapped there forever.

I got my body involved before I lost the will to move entirely, heaving against the side of the tub hard enough that I compressed, squished down until part of me spurted over the lip and hung there. I was nearing exhaustion and my mind was for sure coming apart but I heaved again, squishing another little fold of myself up and over, and did it a few more times until gravity carried me back into the discolored, scratched-up porcelain.

I drew myself up like an inchworm, getting thicker and thicker and then narrowing back down as I pushed forward, getting into something like a rhythm until I was nosing up to the drain and starting to wonder whether the way my flesh had been splitting and recombining was another thing I was going to have to learn to control, but I didn't want to risk slowing down or getting stuck, so I lunged forward as best I could and tried not to brace myself in case the reflex had a corollary in my new form I hadn't encountered yet and I was relieved to find myself splitting and coming back together, squeezing back into the drainpipe with the knowledge that at least some of the functions of my body were still involuntary.

The copper walls pressing in gave me some more surface to channel the thrust of my flailing body, and I worked on that until eventually I found myself lower than I had before, based on my mental map from earlier, with more sewer below me, longer and heavier pipes than I'd encountered before, and I had a powerful urge to dive down that way, and I wasn't in a position to fight any urges right then so I took a plunge into the dark and was astonished by how wide the pipes got and how quickly the urge to dive grew, until I felt the ooze trickling out of a couple places on my skin just like it came leaking from my feet onto Candace's floor and I came to a stop as quick as I could, shoving my tentacles against the walls when I kept sliding, but they turned out to be better suited to acceleration than braking so I had to skid and squish my way to a stop. The narrowness of the passage didn't faze me this time, but the sense of some other entity further down the way and much fucking larger than me sure did. My wounds itched a little more intensely. The presence down the pipe didn't move, or not that I could tell, but sitting and listening gave me a sense of the extent of it by way of some kind of vibration, and it spread out to either side a good deal farther than it initially seemed, and in a straight line, so I took off the way I came, which required my floundering around with clumps of tentacles until they got friction and headed back where the opalescent goo trailing out of me suggested. I came up a feeder line toward a subdivision I was sure I knew just past the limits of a commercial zone with a Target to one side and an abandoned Borders and a Steak-N-Shake the other, the turnoff to the little mall and the highway onramp making a hash of traffic—past that, the development had big brick walls and a first block wholly given over to a roundabout around a big fountain to keep out the noise of the stores. It wasn't exactly the ritziest of all the neighborhoods in town, but I never knew anybody who had their own place out there, either, not even renting with some friends in the middle of the crash. Candace's mom had a house there, though, and I didn't have any trouble recalling the teeth biting into my feet one drunken night not very long ago at all.

I circled the neighborhood looking for the end of

the writhing flesh wall. I couldn't see it again yet, but I could feel it, thicker and closer than it was at the last place, and I kept on, just out of sight, looking for a wrinkle or inconsistency.

I skirted along a just out of its reach until it was clear that it was creeping along the subterranean infrastructure of the subdivision and I was in the footprint of the commercial district, and when I rode a curve in the pipe taking me closer than I'd been keeping I could sense it sending tendrils toward me, sneaking under and around, and remembered the teeth under Candace's pool that didn't prick anyone else, and started to think about myself as a component of these goings-on and not just a target.

The first move was made for me. The pipe ahead of me lost all its depth, filled up by something that moved more like gas than a liquid, drifting in all at once and closing off the distance, flattening the world, and waiting. There was a pull coming off it, something like a voice across a bar that may or may not have been calling my name.

The silence and the stillness stretched on until I started to even doubt that I was really seeing anything —who's to say the dark couldn't get a little bit darker —but then I felt a tingle in my side and a different sort of wetness under me where it wasn't something I could get away from, and it trickled out again like gleaming lymph toward the blockage like the very flat stretch of pipe was on a steep incline, running fast like it was being drawn there, and some part of the dark peeled away from the rest of it, tentatively, and waited for the narrow streams to draw close. It trembled, waiting and tense in contrast with the rest of the mess, while I tried against hope to slow the flow.

Finally the tip of my ooze touched something and I felt a texture that was mostly solid but also felt somehow like a heavy sweaty fog and then a blast of mental static I was in no way equipped to process, like a pressure behind my eyes blocking out my sight and a sudden roar, and a sense of a sprawling form reaching back and up at regular intervals, a parasite grown so deep that it became part of the skeleton, the sprinklers and pool pumps and some sorts of pressure devices.

I turned and fled, well before my senses came back or I had reason to believe they would, back the way I'd come. The ooze that had poured out of me and touched the mobile contamination stiffened and the solidity ran up the little trails into my body and stuck there, a terrifying disruption until it tugged free and slapped the sides of the pipe behind me. The surface seemed now impossibly far above me but I pushed up hard and, pursued by wide booming vibrations, bashed against the underside of a manhole cover. It was raining now, up here at the surface. The rain startled my skin, all the obscure minerals dissolved in it and the oil from the road runoff stinging like a cold wind, and I forced myself up through the holes in the manhole cover in pressure noodles and saw a storm drain through the crosswind blur of passing tires and strained myself in that direction as fast as I could. A set of tires passed over me and I felt it but not as pain, more like a sudden hiccup attack. The pressure slowed my progress but didn't stop it. Soon I was dipping my front end down into the storm drain. It was a bit marvelous how I could feel water down there as well as the manhole cover I was pressing out of, and all of the concrete and asphalt between. The nerves of the fingertips evolved their sensitivity through millions of years of mutational trial-and-error, landing eventually in the place the most precise feeling was most needed, but now I was feeling with that specificity across dozens of yards. The sensation was dizzying.

The new water was shot through with soup and shit, Lysol and painkillers, skin flakes and toothpaste and grass clippings and the long trails of smell and texture leading back the way they came forming a new kind of map, and I was sniffing and tasting before I remembered that I ought to be repulsed by such flows, that that was why we kept them underneath the city. My brain or whatever was doing the job now was focused on the content of the water, that I'd left and that I'd entered, and had a different wiring that could take it all in without switching between.

I worked my way across the street, listening and feeling, pausing when the rumble of wheels got closer so I'd be flat when the cars drove over me, and eventually the tail end of me was sliding across the road and plopping in, and I found the world I could feel dramatically contracted and tried stretching myself out as far as I could without something to squeeze through.

It was a whole different world over this side of the city waterworks. The water was immeasurably more dense with the traces of every home feeding the stream, every slight variation in texture and density and salinity feeding into each of these flows, and the further I stretched myself out, the more I understood how they shifted in a more three-dimensional sense, and back to where they came from, a drainage map that gave me locations but also sometimes skin tones or hair colors or very nearly faces. A picture of the neighborhood the entity clung to began to emerge, along with the one further up the road, and the nearest parts of the commercial strip, with chemicals that burned so sharp even in their limited quantities that I was relieved I wasn't closer to the mall. I wouldn't have been able to detect anything beyond the runoff. I'd found myself in a tangle of pipes closer to the houses they emanated from than where I had been, but I couldn't shake the feeling I had running into the entity or the memory of the teeth that once came up to meet my skin from the inside of its territory. I started winding my way into the neighborhood pipes, stretching myself as long as I could while I went and hearing the mass below me shift in response, until I had worked my way to a block where I was sure Candace lived.

Looking up from below, at a shape very like a street map but reversed, veins and arteries without any flesh and muscle and bone, it was hard to see it all as discrete free-standing structures rather than nodes and distances along the same spiderweb network, above-ground places for nice families to store their baggage in rather than the maze of tubes and pipes and vents maintaining the surface.

All the houses on one side of the dead space I realized must be the road had swimming pools and only one did on the other side. I played the odds, but my memory of my last visit was fevered even before the smudged-glass haze that had come to overlay all my memories from my old body. I put my stretching to work.

I got longer and my world got bigger and bigger until at a certain point it wasn't me growing but the world getting smaller, flexing itself down to accommo-date me, and the shrinking pipes worked around the thinning tendrils of my body. The world was threading me through it, guiding me around some complicated turns and junctions until the subdivision block started to feel like a sweater clinging to my shoulders, a tight but comfortable fit. The water moved around my thin-stretched skin and told me even more—what houses were pulling in water and how much, the variations in pressure and duration, and pretty soon I had a clear map of every sink and swimming pool drain on both sides of the street, one level above the rotting void clinging to the sewage and pressing up until just below most of the drains, and vibrating a bit where I hung down the nearest to it. I settled into the underside of every house on my side of the street.

–

I WAITED FOR THE PRESENCE TO MAKE A MOVE, BUT IT just hung there where I couldn't see it but I felt its tight vibrations. Eventually, the screen door opened above me and a pool heater kicked on with the patio light and that was all the prompt I needed to finally move, let part of myself loose from the hold I'd been keeping it in to push up the pipe, into the drain at the bottom of the pool, and the person I saw through the shimmering water shrug off a mildly unseasonable hoodie and dangle feet in was almost certainly Candace, and though I couldn't figure out how she was involved I knew that if things hadn't started here they certainly escalated here, reached a new stage, and the teeth began to stir under the bottom of the pool and I sensed them now, how many there were waiting when none had been disturbed yet, and so I pulled myself up to as full a height as I could manage and broke for the surface.

With a fold of myself gripping the drain to provide me leverage, I erupted from the surface of the water and then far above, Candace's startle reaction and belated falling-back receding below me until the top of me reached the screen over the deck, bending around the beam and pressing in little squares through the steel mesh but I didn't break through, just held myself there for a second, watching Candace keep her footing for two steps back toward the kitchen but not the third, and unzipped myself from the screen and peeled off the frame and brought myself down all around her.

And on the way down:

I am face-down on the carpet in the afterparty, surrounded by kneeling people I do not know. There is a barrier between me and them, there maybe was even when this gathering was maintaining its veneer of a regular house party possessed of only the secrets and dangers endemic to that form, and I really can't remember why I came. The music suddenly sounds familiar, though, with my ear pressed to the carpet it seems to be oozing from, familiar and alarming, like a certain kind of familial reunion. I don't know it in my head but in my bones, which seem to reverberate with the stuttering pulse, waking up inside of me and beginning an insistent ache that wriggles up into my muscles and I feel old and waking and energized and the haze at the edge of the room pushes into the middle of it and the person next to me slaps their palms on the carpet and slowly lowers their forehead between them and—

—I crashed against the deck, into and through Candace. Something broke inside her, probably a few things, a wave of snapping and bursting I tried to hold all together. The house's windows rattled against their frames and Candace's mom and a man I didn't recognize heaved open the sliding glass door and came through in about the same motion, necessarily off-balance, and tripped and skinned their elbows against the brick before the mass of feelers I frothed out from the pool could wind their way over to them, but they were seized only a moment later by the weave of rubbery flesh, picked up and pinned to the wall of the house where they struggled for the couple of moments before I got my feelers knitted together straightjacket-tight. I curled as much of myself around Candace as I could pull from the pool without breaking my grip around the drain. I tried to whisper to her—*I need to know a few things*—but it didn't seem like she heard me at all. Even with all of my new skills, my ability to speak hadn't improved any.

Candace started to scream and froze with her mouth open and moved her lips around like she was surprised she still could. "Dusty?" she said. "Dusty, what's going on?'

I wish I knew.

'Dusty, is that you? What the fuck happened?"

I wish I knew. I was hoping you could fill in the blanks.

And I tried to give her the short version, but that

curled in on itself and wasn't going to get me anywhere, so I pivoted to a quick question—*Do you know about Alex?*—and she flinched only a little, pretended that she didn't know what I was on about. I saw she was faking it but didn't know what she thought she was keeping from me. This was all a bit much for my social skills at the moment, and so I wrapped a larger part of my body around Candace's foot and pulled hard—

—and I'm gasping my way up to my feet, the music from the floor pumping out of the mouths of everyone in the circle now, and I feel like the only thing separating me from the ground around me is the burning in my stomach, which helps get me up to my feet and out a door I seem to recall entering before and I vomit in the bushes as my recollection starts to fade, and I start to wonder a little what exactly I'm so afraid of and try to tell myself I'm just drunk. I'm certainly that but it's not just that. When I find myself outside my truck with my hand on the door handle I let go, clamber into the bed and curl up in the darkness, reflecting vaguely on my occasional desire to buy a camper shell. I think along those lines because they are those accessible to me, the living room already fading into narcotic semi-memory, but I prop my head up on the edge of the bed and see that I left the door open just a little to the party house, and I sense some motion from inside—

—and Candace was bleeding in my many arms, long cracking fractures and the conversation was not going how I had hoped. Her parents were still struggling though they couldn't move and so I pressed a little harder and they stiffened, they slumped, and I pulled away from them to ask Candace one last time and heard the stone behind me fracturing and water displacing not down into the newly breaking cracks but upward, forced ahead of what else was rushing out, shedding water all over the deck as it drew itself up.

I lurched out of the way, pulling Candace with me away from the massive bulk crashing down into the deck and spilling toward the house even as more of it was falling, smashing through the edge of the roof and the supports for the screen and I found myself only barely past its reach and stretched out to dive faster. I dragged Candace along in a little hammock-sled of my stretched-out skin. The concrete ate into my skin with the speed, thinning it out until Candace's skin pushed through mine and ground against the grain of the deck, leaving little straits of blood wet under my belly and that grew bigger and wider, making the ground a rough coppery slide, but her screams only barely made it through the crash of falling debris and the roar of the erupting pressure blasting it loose, a roar that grew as I fled, so I couldn't tell if Candace fell silent or I just couldn't hear her anymore, and then the roar got louder until there were sparks at my feet, not the blinding nerve of physical contact I had felt underground, not yet, but the magnetic crackle of nearness, and I peeled myself into strips to better pass through the far wall of the screen still mostly standing and anchored to the house, and then through the comparatively wide slats of the wood fence around the yard and I set off dribbling through the grass—

—and something moves in the house, and out in the truck I find the middle ground between my urges to hide in the bed and to keep watching. I let my body slump down with my skull balanced on the steel and watch. The people from the floor file out the door in an unsteady line, blinking like the streetlight a block away is the blazing sun and wandering off in different directions but not random, more like they were heading off toward the same point by different paths. They manage a pretty good pace for how dazed they seem and before long they are fully out of sight. The door to the house is wider open now than before. They left it hanging. It's still like the mouth into something bad but more like a crypt than a yawning monster. They took something out of that house and into the world in a dozen pieces, and my vision starts to get a little staticky, looking after them—

—and eventually the ground sloped down and I strained through the grass into a pool that tasted like all kinds of places, no real connections between them, and a mineral-and-chemical profile that got soupier the deeper I sank. A retention pond, out at the edge of the subdivision where it could be forgotten or landscaped up if expansion came through, a potential plug in the lego set of the subdivision, hanging off on its own for now until it was decided what part if any would get snapped on next. The layers of runoff stung and spun my mind around, less from acridity or toxins than because I couldn't trace them anywhere. They just floated there, sparking the nerve endings in my skin with nothing behind the spark, an alert that didn't point anywhere in particular. When I first hit the water, flush with adrenaline and keeping my ears focused on the rushing presence crashing after me, it only registered as a dim buzz, a tingling on my skin that I could bear, but once the presence seemed to stop following and I lost track of its sounds, the tingling got louder and louder, like the fluorescent lights in a room where you've got nothing else to focus on, buzzing and flashing and alerting me with all the urgency I'd felt blazing through the tunnels of the sewer system, and I curled around myself and tried to wait it out, but the buzzing became a burning and I forced myself down against the soil at the bottom of the pond and then *into* it, finally driving this body into something solid, not through a pipe or door. The relief was gradual at best, and as I worked at stretching my viscous ass down, I got a sense of how deep the contamination from the pond had sunk, most of the way to the limestone-cool water leeching up from the aquifer.

Candace had come apart in the screen, or else she had before, smearing the pool of her blood that had been collecting in the pocket of my skin all over me as I flattened and pulled apart, then wafted off me in thick coils with a brief strong meat smell that was quickly smothered by the water. It had all happened too fast for me to find a shape that would fit with hers, but I was beginning to think there wasn't any such thing, that I had become or was becoming something that could move through the infrastructure of the suburbs that people used, and was somehow produced by all this infrastructure, but with which people could not coexist. Any body I tried to interact with wound up broken or gelatinized or crushed into unrecognizable pulp. I was a new life form, perfectly suited to plumbing and drainage channels, a byproduct of the town that, like much of what got flushed out underneath the houses and lawns, was intolerable to the residents themselves.

I shoved myself down deeper into the dirt, the strands of my body breaking farther apart, now, and it was like water but never quite getting that fluid, so I slowed nearer and nearer a stop and the friction got to be greater than my momentum and what force I was still able to exert and I squished to a suspended stop like a clutch of long icicles hanging down from the surface and I felt something new down there. It wasn't any more straightforward than all the runoff in the pond, not the clarifying connection with nature I had briefly hoped for, but a swirled-together history of the neighborhood, the houses torn down and farmland dug up to make the hole for the pond and all the development around it, long cycles of tilling and sowing punctuated by screams of violent displacement to create the farmland that built this celery-town-cum-suburb, layers of history swirled together in the soil where on the surface they were occulted and illegible.

Meanwhile, the presence wound its way back down into the pipes and circled around me, tightening its pressure with even more mass than I had imagined, drawn from all around, making itself a fence the shape of the neighborhood. How bizarre to feel a sense of panic building about being barred from a subdivision I was never all that fond of.

The corral was tight but didn't get any tighter, settling into an underground wall delineating everything with people in it on its side and just a little slice of the runoff on mine, pinning me downstream, already stunned by the taste and feeling of all the mingled contaminants in the water and growing more so the longer it worked on my skin, so as the underground parts of me were solidifying into long stalactites I pushed the rest of me down behind it painfully slowly, guiding myself inch by inch into the dirt, and the buzzing on my skin didn't get better, in fact got compacted by the soil into a fizzing layer, all of the blended domestic and agricultural and industrial byproducts of the surprisingly long and deep history of this town clinging to me like an exoskeleton, and if my body still worked this way I thought I would probably laugh—if I was becoming what the residents of my beloved hometown couldn't coexist with, couldn't even live alongside, then a part of that was a thick layer of the raw substance of the place—and I tried to feel around for where the presence was but all I got was a feedback screech and a low deep pulse like some kind of bass coming through a very good speaker, coming up from the dirt below the dirt at the bottom of the pond, and I turned my focus downward. My immediate surroundings offered only that threat I didn't understand and all those distant fragile people at the ends of all their various pipes, so though all I expected to feel underneath the ground was a little layer of more ground, increasingly wet toward the aquifer, I kept pushing down and the foreign feeling around my body hardened further and started to take up parts of my skin into itself, and I braced myself to become harder, more carapaced, but instead the melding-in worked the other way, softening and leaching into me.

As the last of my body worked its way down from the water, the sand I broke into at the deepest point got just wet enough for there to be a little bit of movement, a slight current, and I felt myself start to move along with it, not in the quick-twitch slippery way I did through the pipes but a slow unsteady flapping like an octopus trying to swim in a vat of vegetable oil, and I tried to push it to go faster but that didn't move the needle one way or the other. I spread out through the sand at the speed of sand. When you're working in a warehouse, you perceive everything around you at warehouse speed; when you're following sand dissolved in very little water you start to think at the speed of sludge.

The world outside my damp pit sped up around me. I ground to very nearly a halt and the parts that first felt like a shell and then an injection now felt like stinging rods running through my flesh and poking out through my ends, innumerable fingernails of the narrow epoxy of history, not appendages I could do anything with but hang draped over while the world outside my pond accelerated beyond the noises and traces I could follow into a blurry din like a train full of impossibly loud cicadas cosmically far away, a nasal white noise that thinned out until I wasn't even listening to it, may have been hearing but was by no means processing over the heavy thrum of the soil and something even lower that I was just beginning to feel, but that beginning felt like something I had heard before.

I relaxed myself as best I could to try to go along with the sludge, fully ease myself into the earthen pace of things, and found that I was already expanding outward, not in streaks or strips but a dim dank cloud that I could see the eventual shape of, a light bulb swelling underneath the pond until it became a bulbous subterranean bowl, a shape reaching to come into being. I already couldn't tell how long I'd been down there, and the thinner and flakier the tissue of the world became, the more it let me slide through it and with less resistance, the more my senses came into alignment with all the flesh that delivered them to me. Through a long and gritty descent, following along the troughs carved ahead of me by my history-shell claws, over which I continued to exert no influence, I came to believe that I was arriving at a final form after the several I had felt over startlingly few years, and began to think of even that method of measuring a life—years, moments, discrete periods of transcribable time condensable to high-lights and rememberable as stories—as the remnants of an overground life that now lay behind me, to which I would never and would eventually want to never return, until—

The world slows back down as I break through, ramps back into a time that already feels foreign to me, but the urge to spread myself out, become broader, takes a firm hold as I burst into a new layer of the soil that blinds me like tube-light and pushes me to re-enter the world on something like its own terms. I can't tell what sort of medium I am moving through—it must be some kind of dirt, or maybe aquifer limestone, but it feels like air and looks like light and all I feel is the absence of the confused pres-sure from the pondwater, the breaking-away of all the various signals setting a nervous fire all along my skin, and it's a soaring sort of relief that doesn't help me understand anything in particular but I am possessed by a further push toward expanding myself, and I go with that urge, working myself out in all directions until I feel something, but it takes a while even by my new reckoning, and it feels like a whole new scale than

I'd felt before, even at my most expansive, and the feeling is pleasantly like teetering with my toes over the edge of a very high rooftop.

My sight begins to return and it seems I've followed the less-occupied parts of the water table out away from the pond and its subdivision, and when my senses get a little more clear I find I've already wrapped some dense parts of myself around joints in the plumbing. I come into awareness of my surroundings with a sharp jolt of panic, but I wait a few seconds like drawing breath and sense that the presence I'd encountered in the pipes is still locked into its grip around the subdivision, and once panic subsides and I'm sure I'm not immediately threatened by it, I feel how much larger I am than I was before and my fear of that other presence loses some of its teeth. I am becoming a presence myself. It lurks over on its side of town and I start a little liquid stroke around what seems to be becoming my territory, getting a feel for where the water moves more and where less within its sand and dirt and rock, where I could get myself near enough to the storm drains to start spilling myself over into them, back into the sewer system, and I try it all along the length and width of my spread-out body, winding my way into pipes and drains and under houses. The pressing need to expand as far out as I can gives way to its opposite. I start to pull myself in within the borders I've established so far, doubling under myself and taking my time about it, gradually giving myself a clearer picture of all the runoff of three or four streets and the bodies it's coming off of.

It's all familiar but like it's changed some, like the town has some more years and buildup hanging onto it now, and I'm coming at things from underneath but behind as well, and I can't quite tell which of the people I feel in their castoff are ones I know. Probably not many of them.

I concentrate myself in a central point directly underneath a couple of houses where I'm already the strongest, pulling in from my edges without surrendering that territory so that I can maintain my understanding of the world at least that far, and start to listen to who is up there. I find one house in particular that's pretty fully populated and pretty young, ten or twelve people experiencing a weekend sort of altered consciousness regardless of what day it actually is, a temporal displacement as like mine as can be hoped for with their very human limitations, and most of them feel as different from me as they are, closed off residents of an entirely different form of being, but some feel more open to me somehow, vibrating on some dangerously sympathetic frequency. Their bodies reflect something of mine, even if they haven't begun to change in the ways I suddenly understand that they will, that they must as surely as a misprogrammed protein must develop into cancer, gripping into the tissue around it and making a fleshy world for itself, and I push up to meet them.

Movement comes easier for me now. The parts of

me I've worked through storm drains and the like thread their way toward the house I decide on without much input from me at all, leaving me free to focus on the process of filtering through the ground and then the foundations of the house. I leave the nail-like prongs of myself, collected from the history of the town in the pond, driven into the concrete underside of the house and they settle there, waiting for me in my charge upward. I find grass and wood and steel and infiltrate this house of merriment quickly, misting up under the floor and settling into the threads of the carpet and waiting until the music and the mood align with me even more, the beginnings of a slow slide into unconsciousness, and I seethe right up into the living room and into your waiting brain, an approach that I didn't know until just now I have been preparing for all this time, and if you'll just listen I know that I will pull you down into myself, oh yes, but what's more, you will barely think to fight me on the way down.

ABOUT THE AUTHOR

Mark grew up in Florida and now lives in eastern Kansas. This is his third book. Find the latest at mutantcircuit.com.

The Organization is Here to Support You - Charlene Elsby

Without the organization, Clarissa Knowles would have nowhere else to go. That is, unless she can make it to Dick's house, the professor she's been talking to online. Haunted by her failed relationship with Maurice (the existentialist), and the deaths of her parents, can Clarissa shake off the values of the organization, pack up her cat – and go?

The Organization is Here to Support You is an existential bureaucratic horror satire in the tradition of Franz Kafka, J.G. Ballard, and Sayaka Murata.

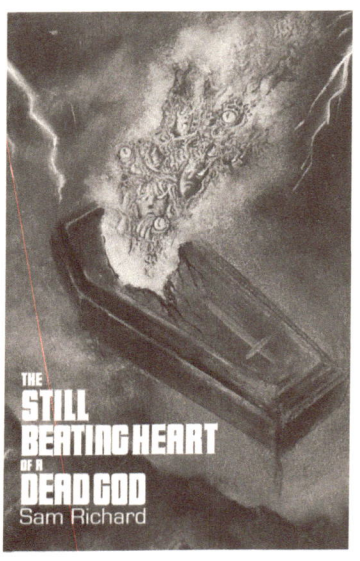

The Still Beating Heart of a Dead God - Sam Richard

A drunk widower wanders through an endless, abandoned mall while the war machine marches.

90s queer metalheads repeatedly try to burn down a regenerating church.

Denizens of a punk house are confronted with the reality of what happened to their missing roommate.

An artist with acidic bodily fluids finds another like him.

With *The Still Beating Heart of a Dead God* Award-Winning author Sam Richard returns with eleven new stories exploring the raw honesty of grief, isolation, brokenness, and desperation through weird horrors ranging from body to cosmic to existential and beyond.

Love Skull - Emma Alice Johnson

Pizza cults! Barn ghouls! Carpet zombies! Skulls and kisses!

A background skull from a popular 80s horror novel comes to life and becomes obsessed with the book's reader. Two women fall in love as a giant monster destroys the town around them. Friends band together to haul their BFF's corpse to the ocean for the ultimate funeral-by-shark.

This collection includes the New York Times-mentioned "5 Ways to Kill Your Rapist on a Farm" and 11 other stories that blend horror, sci-fi, weird, and romance into a unique mix from award-winning author Emma Alice Johnson.

CORNUCOPIA

CORNUCOPIA

A Fractured Cities Tale

Alek L. Cristea

DEDICATION

To all those who grew up in places they didn't fit and set off on journeys to find their home: be it place or people.

ONE

B efore we start with the story proper, let me first set the scene. For the scene is the story and the story is the scene, each so tangled with the other as to be indispensable to the other's existence. Imagine, if you will, a city of zealots and extremists, of unbelievable beliefs and every excess man can dream of. Beliefs in gods of old and idols of the still living. Beliefs in things long lost and things newly born. Excess of the flesh and denial. Excess of pride and abnegation.

Imagine, a city where the only crime is moderation.

Imagine, Cornucopia.

Imagine then, a place nestled at the heart of the city, lost in backstreets away from the riot of the main thoroughfares, the outside lit only with a simple, single oil lamp. A place so at odds with the city it should not have been able to exist. A place illegal for its name alone. A place—somehow—allowed to stand even as the city shifts, changes, and grows.

Let me welcome you to *Moderation*, a small bar off the beaten track, away from the eyes of the starving and the prodigal. A small place, really, unremarkable for all but its name, painted elegantly on a sign just slightly off of lovely enough to compliment the handwriting. Unremarkable — with its wooden walls and fireplace and small, cosy tables — but for the man standing behind the stained bar, a strip of cloth in hand as he finished drying yet another glass.

You see, the Bartender of *Moderation* was not, unlike his establishment, unremarkable. No-one who lived within the city remembered when he had arrived, no-one knew where he had come from, as though he had simply appeared, him and his bar that never seemed to close. He had eyes that looked as old as the city, brown like sunrises through the smog, too keen to belong to a man who poured drinks and cleaned glasses, too sharp for the casual smile he always wore. None that came to the bar dared look long into them.

They said that if you did you would spill your life story.

You would lose your faith.

You would never look upon the city and its inhabitants the same.

They said there was only madness to be found in his eyes.

But the Bartender didn't mind that his patrons never made eye contact. Between you and me, I think he preferred it that way, finding an uncomfortable intensity in those windows to the soul.

His hands were just as disconcerting, too calloused to be as elegant as they were, too deft to be the result of a life behind a bar. They were like a spectacle in themselves, quick but precise as he poured drinks and cleaned glasses, never stopping, never resting, as though they were possessed of a spirit that demanded they were ever moving.

His name was *Bartender*, for no-one ever bothered to ask. No-one — truly — wanted to know. There is a power to names, you see, and even this mad city knows that. To know the Bartender's name would not, it was said, gift power over him to any who learnt it. Oh no, to know his name was to know too much. In his name, they said, much like in his eyes, waited only madness. Or, depending on your perspective, reason.

Our story began in earnest away from *Moderation*, away from Cornucopia itself, in another city as dangerous as this one though its weapons of choice were not excess and idolatry but close-mindedness and the worst brand of intolerance. In Cornucopia proper, this tale's chapter begins on one particularly rainy day, the sky weeping over the aftermath of a terrible fight in between the Priests of Gluttony, and the Starveling's Chosen, the emaciated bodies of the latter still carpeting the ground a few streets away from our bar. The fat priests had made short work of the assailants that had shouted insult after insult even as they struggled to remain standing, barely more than skin-clothed skeletons. But neither that fight, nor the endless faction wars that wreck the city's core, play a part in our story.

The rain, however, is of utmost import, for without it, the young man would not have sought a place to dry himself. His dripping wheelchair creaked as he pushed himself inside *Moderation*, to dry warmth and shelter. A few looks went his way, but save for the chair, he was an unremarkable young man. The cut of his clothes was nowhere near fine enough to mark him as a disciple of Vanity, but he looked far from poor or unkempt. There was no sign of any faith around his neck or wrist or wrapped about his head, no make-up at the corner of his eyes to identify what idol he might worship.

He seemed, in fact, the very personification of moderation, perhaps even more than the Bartender with sharp eyes and butterfly hands. Though here, inside the bar of that very name, he did not draw looks, did not garner the unwanted attention he had outside.

The first thing the Stranger noticed upon wheeling to a stop at a lowered corner of the bar, were the rules hanging behind the Bartender, whose keen eyes were not-quite-staring at him.

Everything in Moderation, the first line read, chalk-clumsy writing on an old, tattered board.

1- Everyone must have a drink

2- No-one gets drunk

3- Beliefs and faiths are not to be discussed

4- No excessive behaviours of any kind will be tolerated

These seemed, to the Stranger, like the most bizarre set of rules he had ever seen. But then, this city he had entered only earlier that day, was the most disconcerting he had ever witnessed. He was well travelled, especially given his age and condition, and Cornucopia was the most unsettling city he had visited to date. He had been asked, upon disembarking the airship, if there was any vice or faith he wished to declare so he could be pointed to the right faction. When he had said he was only passing through, he was given the address of a neutral hotel and sent on his way with the condescension of those who believe their faith or lifestyle is the only truth in a world of lies.

How the Stranger came to be lost in the streets of Cornucopia is the well-known story of a foreigner in foreign land. Through what he would grow to think as fate, but might well have simply been luck, he had found *Moderation* in his time of need.

"What drink do you want?" The Bartender sounded somewhere in between gruff and gentle, a voice neither nearly sharp enough to match his cheekbones, nor soft enough for the tone he used.

The Stranger thought about saying he didn't want a drink, but he had seen the rules and didn't fancy being sent back into the downpour. "The kind of drink that helps you find the lost," he said, perhaps a little too much of the last city he had visited clinging to him at the edges.

The Bartender perked up, eyes twinkling with excitement he never displayed when pouring beer after whisky after rum after beer—an endless cycle of mostly brown drinks in tones that sometimes matched his eyes, sometimes matched the wood, and sometimes matched the dark blond of his hair.

"It's not an easy thing to come by, a drink that answers questions that cannot be asked," he replied, setting down both glass and cloth, fingers carrying on their dance on the counter. His eyes rested on the Stranger's left shoulder, where the wool of his coat was bobbling in patterns that might have reminded the Bartender of constellations if Cornucopia's sky had not been permanently shrouded in smog.

"Then just a drink to soothe a soul," the Stranger replied, running a hand through shoulder-length hair, scattering raindrops all around him.

The Bartender made a thoughtful sound, fingers playing an invisible piano. "But the question is, Stranger, what does your soul taste like? Is it dark as those who bathe only in blood, or light like the angels of the Cathedral that kneel and pray until they die? No, no, if your soul was as simple as that, Stranger, this is not where you would have ended up." The Bartender turned around, humming a tune only he knew as he slid his hand alongside his bottles until it came to rest on one, tucked in a corner and a little dusty. It would have been a truly beautiful bottle if not for the crooked label and faded lettering; it would have looked ugly if not for the elegant curve of the neck and the colour of the glass, blue as the Stranger's eyes. The Bartender carried on humming, taking his time selecting a glass. He chose a simple one: to complement the liquor and moderate its mesmerising gleam, and poured a measured dose, deposited with precision in front of the Stranger.

Their eyes met, only an instant before the Bartender looked away again, but the Stranger felt a pull. His fingers found the glass, but his eyes never left the Bartender.

"Perhaps you could help me?" he asked, voice a little halting and shy, at odds with his bold eyes.

"I'm here to pour the drinks."

"Could I ask you a question?"

The Bartender glanced over at the chalkboard and scowled. He considered in that moment adding a fifth rule. *No questions.*

To my knowledge, he never has.

"You can *ask*."

The Stranger hesitated, torn in between the friendly demeanour and rejecting words. He brought the liquor to his lips and took a tentative sip. He had expected it to burn, but it was smooth, sliding down his throat like a bird in flight slipping from one current to the next.

"I'm looking for someone," he started, digging out a folded sheet of paper from inside his jacket.

It was unremarkable, but in *Moderation*, the very presence of that paper was like a beacon for attention. It had clearly been folded and unfolded many times by the very hands that now held it, its edges frayed, its creases tearing, its colour twisted from white, or perhaps cream, to an unpleasant yellow. Its presence here did not break any rules, but it struck the chord of past stories that ended in tears and future ones with uncertain conclusions, of doors slammed painfully shut and those about to crack open onto new beginnings.

Little did the patrons know that this story had started a little over a year ago, when another young man had set foot within Cornucopia, his footsteps not so lucky to find *Moderation*.

"Do you think you might have seen him?" the Stranger asked, laying the unfolded sketch on the bar. It was a stunning thing, truly, that spoke of natural and trained talent coming together to render a masterpiece of likeness, as though the Stranger's subject might turn his head to face whoever was looking at the drawing, a smile animating an otherwise serious face.

The Bartender glanced at the picture, fingers reaching for the paper but never quite touching it. It was not a face he had seen inside his bar, but it was a face he had heard of. Too handsome to be unremarkable, the sketch captured the essence of the loose, blond curls that fell about his face in perfect waves, depicted in noticeable detail the full, inviting lips.

In Cornucopia, it was the kind of face that would get one noticed.

That could get one worshipped.

After all, this was the city that built idols out of the living, even the unwilling, so long as their beauty or charisma was remarkable enough.

"He never came here. Never saw him. But I can tell you where to find him."

The Stranger looked up sharply, blue eyes dancing with desperate hope. "And where might that be?"

TWO

The Stranger had not waited for the rain to stop. Knowledge was power like a bolt of urgency, the fear of endings painted in shades of red. Knowledge was what he had sought, but gaining it came at a price. He did not rush through the city, the roads too unpredictable and his arms tired, but he made steady progress, avoiding the strange people he crossed on the streets. Some dressed solely in blue, the cloth they wore loose and baggy, some clad only in dark skin-tight outfits. There were some that went about on their hands, laughing in their upside-down world. He saw sights he had no words to describe, caught glimpses of acts that rewrote his understanding of the world.

And wherever he went, wheels creaking a little, he was *Stranger*.

When street vendors called out they named him so, when the criers of faiths and idols reached out to him, it was the name they promised freedom from.

Stranger.

But the Stranger had been just that all his life. A stranger to a family that had failed to understand much about him, and a stranger in all his travels.

The instructions from the Bartender had been thorough, and the Stranger had noted them down, hands scribbling fast in his journal as the man spoke, his voice paced and yet the information almost too quick to follow. Cornucopia was a maze of endless backstreets, twists, and dead ends. The Bartender had warned him that there were places to avoid, and places never to step foot in. He had been tempted to ask what the difference was but the glint in the Bartender's eyes as he stared at a point past the Stranger had given it away. There were simply places in Cornucopia one did not find one's way back from.

What might have been dusk—or could have been dawn, who, truly, could tell here? —was settling over the city when he finally made it to the entrance of the Cathedral of Idols.

The Stranger wondered, as he craned his neck and failed to see the top, whether this was less a building and more a city within the city. The front doors were tall as four men, wide as ten, but in the imposing metal had been cut smaller doors, their frosted glass promising only light inside, letting nothing else escape the massive structure.

The Stranger was struck with anxiety at the sight: the overdone facade of wrought metal and carved stone, the clock face, halfway up, displaying an impossible time. The whole thing was devoid of windows save for a single, massive one above the clock from which lights in a thousand colours poured out only to be swallowed by the smog.

And above that... the Stranger did not know, for he could not see, but dread loomed down upon him.

He looked away from the dizzying height, neck sore and he rubbed it worse as he tried to make it better. Sighing, he returned his attention to the glass doors. Two guards, if they could be called such, stood at the entrance. One was dressed in severe grey: a perfectly tailored uniform that spoke of order, of the belief that each thing had a place and only one. Embroideries matching the buttons matching the colour of his eyes. And at the corner of said eyes, the two ends of a perfectly weighted scale hung, painted or tattooed with absolute precision.

The other was opposite in every way: hair wildly spiked and painted in a rainbow, a tongue sticking out painted over bright lips. The clothes were a riot of colours, mismatched patchwork trousers and shirt, boots so bright a yellow they might have been attempting to stand in for the absent sun. A dozen necklaces rang like bells and at the corner of bright green eyes curled flowers like the Stranger had never seen.

"What is your business, Stranger? Seeking refuge from the wet is not reason enough to enter these hallowed halls," the Gaudy Guard declared, overacting a bow.

I seek someone, he almost said. Had his steps not lead him to *Moderation* first, he would have spoken those very words and seen the doors barred to him. But instead, he said: "I seek to pay respect."

"Ooh," the Gaudy Guard cooed. "And to whom do you pay respect? I see no mark upon your skin, *Stranger*, no jewel at your neck or fingers?"

"My respects are my own to give," the Stranger said, repeating the Bartender's words.

The Immaculate Guard moved then, stiff as the hands of the clock that loomed above.

"You speak the words of the Idols. Please, follow me."

The voice was as devoid of tone as the outfit was of flaws, unsettling to the Stranger though perhaps less so than the guard who backflipped away from him with a grin that twisted their make-up covered face in unnatural ways.

On the other side of frosted glass, the hall was too much and yet too little. Too large with too few furnishings. Too warm with too little air. Darkly coloured and yet somehow too gaudy with far too little taste intertwining the two. It was an assault on the Stranger's senses, a condensed version of the city in which he felt he might drown. The chandelier that hung from the ceiling, bathed everything in almost blinding light after the semi-darkness outside, discordant music mixing with beatific voices. There were too few shadows and too few silences, enveloping the entrance in the kind of frenetic energy usually reserved for those whose minds had been twisted by substances into a riot of things that should not be.

The Immaculate Guard led the Stranger into a smaller side corridor, so sharply in contrast with the hall that the Stranger wondered if it had been a mirage. The corridor was odd in its own way, stretching into infinity, each side lined with doors perfectly equidistant from one another, all darker brown than the wood-panelled walls, and each with a plaque in their centre. All, that is, save for the very first door on the left. It bore only a symbol in the shape of an open book. The Immaculate Guard opened the door and motioned for the Stranger to enter.

"May the Idols watch over you."

And just like that the Stranger was left alone in the room, extreme in its starkness with white walls and a white floor and no windows, only a desk and rusting chair, and upon the desk, the biggest tome the Stranger had ever seen. He hesitated, not for the first time in his travels, but, he hoped, for the last time. There was something ominous about the volume, about what he thought it would hold. The answer to the question he had asked in other cities might well lay within these pages. But there is a weight to truth. A weight that pulls one in just as it pushes away.

Danger.

To know the truth is to have power over one's own reality, but to hold the truth at bay is to hold power over one's heart. A trade-off not easily made.

The Stranger could choose to turn away, convince his heart and mind that the answer was not waiting within. That he had run out of luck and finally the trail had gone cold. He could turn and wheel back to the hotel and sleep, and tomorrow he could take an airship and go home, pretending that all this had been the folly of youth. He could wield this power over his heart and hope it stayed, hope that as time went and his heart hardened that the spell would not break. That he would not look back to this moment with painful regret.

Or the Stranger could choose to move forward, reach a hand and push the chair out of the way, shoulder clicking as he wheeled himself under the desk. He could marvel at the book in front of him, at the feat of the nameless *something* that kept it bound together. Kept it from ever being full.

Magic, some said.

Faith, whispered others.

Not that it mattered, for, as with most things, it was not the how that mattered, but simply the what-it-could-do.

The Stranger could choose to lay a hand on the book, to feel a shudder run through him. He could choose to close his eyes and think of the one he had lost. The one he longed for. He could do as the Bartender had instructed and when he opened his eyes again, the answer to his question, the object of his quest would be at last revealed to him. Close but out of reach.

The Stranger hesitated, aware of the ramifications of his choices. Aware of the dangers of this city as he had been aware in the last city and would be aware in any city after that. And he was afraid, for there were many things a sickly young man was not equipped to defend himself against.

But fear was not the only thing at play. Something else. Something greater burned inside the Stranger. Something built of a friendship as old as breath, of its evolution discovered at the cusp of growing up. And that something won. As well it should.

It won, as the Bartender knew it would. As all who had met the Stranger and the Idol before they were separated would have known. It won, and the Stranger laid a hand on the book, letting his future open beneath his touch.

THREE

Hours passed—the Bartender now heavy with the knowledge of where he had sent the Stranger, though lightened by the certainty that he could not have turned the young man from his path—before a familiar face walked into *Moderation*. Greasy black hair pulled back and dark brown skin streaked with oil where it showed from under baggy, shapeless clothes. A Mechanic: one of the many worshippers of the new machines that were slowly but surely taking over the city. Though to the Bartender she was more than that, she was a Regular: a face that marked the passing of time as steadfastly as a clock.

He did not fail to notice the lack of tools at her belt or the slump of her shoulders. Grief-stricken hollowness had replaced the light in her eyes. It was not a rare sight within *Moderation,* where the lost and the hurting came to find solace. The city was always eager to take the lost in its embrace only to swallow them whole, holding onto them so tight that flight was never an option, only death, slow and steady as a ticking clock. Each second a moment closer to suffocation, to succumbing to excesses, to paying in blood for a faith in false gods.

The Bartender, though he never seemed to leave his bar, had seen all the wounds the city could inflict. Boys and girls and those that were neither, broken in back alleys at the hands of those who worshipped the act of taking what was not theirs. People filling their bodies with poison in the name of a god made up during a hallucination. He had seen girls that were in fact boys cut their wrists when the faith of their parents painted them as monsters, and boys who were in fact girls giving their whole selves to the worship of looks, letting their sharp, beautiful minds rot in favour of glittering eyes and perfect lips. He had seen people starve as their neighbours ate themselves to death. He had seen beings rotted by drugs whilst their family died for lack of taking any. He had seen those who had found a noose, or a gun, or a window high enough, and ended it all when their faith, their vice, their *everything* had lost its appeal or rejected them.

The wound in the Regular's eyes was loud, an endless scream of loss and fear that reached all the way to her soul. She walked straight to the bar, eyes on nothing at all as she took her usual seat, feet remembering the way, her hands finding their usual grip on the counter as she twisted into place.

"What drink do you want?" the Bartender asked, as he always did, for it was the rule. She would talk only if she chose to. He was only a man, and the pains of others were not often in his power to soothe with more than just a drink and the offer of an ear.

"The u- No. I need something new. Something sharp. Something that hurts and makes you feel alive," the Regular said, rubbing her hands together to get the grease out of her skin—a fruitless endeavour with no water or soap.

The Bartender turned to his bottles, a tune on his lips as he pondered them, toyed in his mind with a few, imagining the sound of the alcohol pouring, the feel of it on the tongue and down the throat. At last he climbed onto a footstool and reached for a bottle from the top shelf. It was a tacky marvel of glass, shaped in the idea of a flower, though it was clear the artist had never seen such a thing in his life. The alcohol was a lurid pink, so bright as to be offensive in the muted decor of *Moderation*, so the bartender selected an opaque glass to mute it before handing it to the Regular. She looked at it with a dubious scowl but brought it to her lips anyway, if with visible apprehension.

Everyone knew the Bartender always gave you exactly what it was that you asked for, but that was usually when one realised that what had been asked for might not have been what was wanted.

She hesitated, the edge of the glass resting on her bottom lip, her dark amber eyes lost on something no-one else could see. They were empty of tears, as she was empty of herself, lost and all but frozen in time. She wanted to die. She wanted to feel alive. That was what she had asked for. A pain that made you feel alive, a sharp contrast to her pain that made her want to die. Silence fell in *Moderation*, as though all present knew the importance of that drink, the significance of how it was held, poised, like someone teetering on the edge, caught in between.

The Regular knocked back the drink in one go, her head tilting back until every drop of the lurid liquid was drained, the pink slipping off the opaque surface with eagerness and ease. It burned down her throat, down into her body, robbing her of air so she could not gasp though her hand flew up to her throat. But the pain was warm like a fire, like a promise. Like a kiss ended too soon. The pain blossomed, opening like the impossible flower that had held the liquor, and the Regular felt something new, a shudder running through her. Her eyes slipped out of focus and then back in, and she blinked, as though seeing the bar for the very first time. The Bartender didn't quite smile at her, but it was a near thing, not so much present on his lips as it was at the corner of his eyes.

"You serve magic," she said, carefully placing the glass down, instead of slamming it as she did with her usual choice.

"I serve only what is asked for," he replied, taking the glass and slipping it next to the others that needed cleaning. He did not touch the coins she had laid on the table for he had not asked for a price yet.

"Well it sure did the trick. I don't like feeling like everything is pointless. Still don't like *knowing* everything is a lie though." She tried catching his eye then, but the Bartender was skilled at avoiding her, though he gifted her a single meeting of gaze, barely more than a beat. The Regular knew the Bartender enough to know the gesture as the gift it was. She did not try again. She fell silent, fingers tracing patterns on the wood in front of her as the Bartender carried on his dance of cleaning and tidying. She wanted, *needed*, him to ask, though she knew he would not.

She wondered if he could, or if part of the strangeness that bound him to this place made it so he could not ask others to speak the words that would inevitably pour from their lips. She knew she would talk, despite telling herself she would wait for someone to ask, someone to notice. She had known that coming here would undo her, undo a resolve forged in grief and disillusion. Perhaps, the Regular thought, it was exactly why her feet had led her here, knowing that she stood too close to the edge, that the blade of a knife had too suddenly become an enchanting thing. Her soul ached and bled, but her feet did not want for her the ending she had contemplated.

"I'm no longer a Mechanic," she spoke, barely an audible whisper over the hum of conversations. She wasn't looking at the Bartender anymore, instead shaping imaginary cogs on the bar. "I... I got exiled."

Exiled. Sent away from the Mechanic territory, from the buildings and factories in which they made their home, to never again be welcomed in the places where they ate and drank and *made*. Mechanics were always *making*. Small robots and towering ones, little things that were more toys than anything, and others that could have changed the course of some people's lives if they had not been so keen to keep it all to themselves. *Their* possessions, worshipped like a thousand tiny gods, unwilling to share even a portion of their craft with those who did not share their faith.

Exiled. Cut off from everything that had made up her core: her gears and cogs and batteries, her small altars of broken parts. Her *faith* ripped from her, leaving her marked as unworthy.

The Bartender turned to her then, setting down glass and cloth with so little sound that it might not have happened at all, eyes dancing not on her shoulder but on the curls of hair at her temple, where a streak of grease sharpened her cheekbone in a beautiful accident.

"Where will you go now?" He did not ask how it had come to be, felt no true curiosity towards it, for what use was the past to him? What had happened had happened. There was no undoing the reality of what the Regular had experienced. No pulling back the thin threads of time that kept the world heading ever onwards. What had happened was set in stone as surely as the foundations of the city. What *was* could not be unmade. What *would be* was where potential waited.

The Regular let out a breath, sharp, almost exasperated though those who might have been listening would have been hard pressed to tell if it was at herself or at the Bartender. It was not the question she had wanted. She would have to make herself speak if she wanted to talk. She could not expect the man with butterfly hands to do it all for her.

"I don't know," she answered, grease-stained hands running over her hair in restless, anxious gestures. "Where *can* I go? The Factories were *everything*. Home and hearth.

Parent. Tutor. What am *I* without them but a loose cog with no purpose?"

"Perhaps," the Bartender started, reaching for another bottle and pouring another drink, this one brown as the Regular's skin, its aroma so strong that she smelled it before the glass was in front of her. "What you should be asking is, what are the Factories without *you*? Much damage can be done by a single, missing cog."

She scoffed and did not take the drink. She did not know what this one promised and did not dare try. There was always a risk in accepting a drink you had not asked for, though in *Moderation* it did not come from fear of what might come after said drink had been drunk, but more so in what would happen during. Her first drink had brought pain and life but, although she trusted the Bartender, the Regular was not sure what he had in store for her now.

"I have no purpose," she insisted, and he could see it in her eyes when he stole a glance at them whilst they were otherwise distracted.

In those hollowed eyes, the Bartender saw a possibility, a hand with which to reach out into the world. He saw a way to gift back the purpose that had been taken, for crimes undoubtedly false. For what counted as sins within the varied faiths might well have been the tenets of another. What was an aberration to one might have been someone's chosen excess, the entire purpose of their whole lives. In the pain held as tightly as the Regular's renewed desire to live, the Bartender saw a chain of events, causes and consequences. All started when a boy with blond hair had stepped off an airship, sent away to get lost in the bowels of a city that would too readily enslave him. All leading to this moment, to the Regular slumped in her stool, shoulders heavy with no purpose to carry. Eyes lost in the realisation that what she had—and perhaps, in that strange way people sometimes clung to the false, still did—believed in was not what she had thought it was. It was not permanent. It was not, in fact, any more right than the belief of another. It had not offered a true release from Cornucopia and had not stayed as the eternal Haven—her forever-place in this city, her forever-safety in a world so dangerous—she had expected it to be.

"Drink up," the Bartender said. "And I will give you a purpose."

Her eyes were sharply on him and her hand even more sharply on the glass. The brown liquid tasted of the future, of possibilities.

Of purpose.

FOUR

The Regular had never been to these parts of town, not that she remembered anyway. Perhaps when she had been so small that she could not be trusted to let go of her parents' hands. Perhaps when she had fled the darkness in blood-stained whites, her memories of everything *before* and *during* nothing but a haze. Perhaps before her hands had first found cogs and gears and purpose in the company of an older woman, a Mechanic, who showed her the light. Showed her the way. Until that way, too, had gone dark, plunging her back into the nothing of before. Only now she was not a child. Only now she was aware of the lacking emptiness in her life.

Here, the Regular was unlike her epithet. She was *stranger* at best, and *intruder* at worst, for her clothes still marked her as part of what she had been before. She was not solely someone who did not belong to the city but belonged only to a part of it. She'd had her place, like her gears, and now she was venturing into a machine that was not hers. She did not know it, did not understand how its cogs worked, how to oil them and set them in motion. But as she was now Exiled instead of Mechanic, she carried on, blinkering herself to the sights of the city that left her queasy with dread.

In the Mechanics, everything had its place. Order reigned. Order in behaviours as well as in tidiness. Rules were strict and enforced. Rules were obeyed. They shaped every breath, every thought. They had been her everything, followed—she had thought—to the very letter. Until, of course, the day her mind had strayed and taken her hands with it. Until she had wanted more and been left with less instead.

But that is not our story. Hardly a story worth telling, the Regular would tell you, though what she would mean is that her pain is not to be a spectacle. It is for her and her alone. That moment time will never forget, that pain carved deep into her soul, is not meant to be seen and exposed. It shapes her quietly from the inside, her most prized possession in a city that had taken everything else.

The Regular walked along cobbled streets and those made only of beaten earth. She walked past buildings that tried to stretch to the sky, and passed those that hardly dared to grow higher than the ground itself. She did not look at the people who walked the streets, for she knew she would find no purpose in them, no new belief to be followed, only the repeated awareness that there was something wrong, that all of them thought they were right when she had come to the realisation that, in Cornucopia, such a thing was impossible.

Right and wrong were words for other cities. They did not belong here, in this city of madness. The Regular did not think she had ever understood their meaning any less than she did now.

Still, here she was, so far from home, although home was forbidden and barred and home no longer, meandering in this city of dreams and nightmares, of angels and daemons. Here she was, on an errand taken on in exchange for purpose and a tab wiped clean and kept so for three months. It seemed an infinitely small price to pay. *I need you to find someone*, the Bartender had said and the Regular had listened, the taste of purpose still sharp on her tongue.

I need you to find someone. A someone looking for another someone in a place where the named wear masks and the nameless are lost. I need you to find him, perhaps even them.

She had asked, then, what she was to do when she had found them, these two mysterious someones. The Bartender had given no names, saying only that she would know the first when she met him and he, in turn, would know the second. His answer had been vague and held mostly in the half smile he had slanted her way. She had not been able to decipher it as benevolence or threat, but she had read the promise written on his lips. A promise for idle hands that had not known idleness in so long, a purpose for a mind too keen to be left unoccupied.

She had accepted and he had wiped her tab and poured her another glass, the same liquid, dark as her skin. And for a second time that night, the Regular had tasted purpose. Had tasted meaning. A goal. A *something* to fill the emptiness the Mechanics had ripped inside of her.

The walk to her destination was long, though in this city shielded from the sun, almost blind to the cycle of day and night, she was barely aware of time.

The Regular arrived not at the overlarge doors the Stranger had come to, but at a side entrance the Bartender had given her direction to. Her quarry here was different. She too might be seeking someone, but she could not find them the way the Stranger had. As such, her entrance needed to be different. Informal. Secret. The Stranger had needed to be seen. The Regular was a shadow slipping in. She belonged here just as much as the Stranger, but her Mechanic's clothes, even free of her tools, shaped her as other. Already moulded as she was, she did not belong in a place where more moulds waited to be filled. Moulds she could never fit into.

The door was, as the Bartender had told her, left open to let in some air. And it did, much as the Regular had been told, lead into the kitchens for the building, where the worshippers worked in the cacophony of cooking implements, each action accompanied by a small, muttered prayer to their ingredients. They did not speak to each other, though their hands and eyes seemed to have a language all their own, and it was only the pans and cutlery and cooking stations that filled the silence with something other than eerie reverence.

The Cooks did not see her, focused only on the subject of their faith as she slipped by at the edges of the room, wondering to herself if she too had once looked like one of them, a being lost to everything but madness, engrossed only in the belief that shaped their lives and guided all their actions. Had her eyes been so full of mad fervour as she stood at her station and worked with her gears?

The Regular did not look back when she left the kitchens behind. It was, perhaps, in that moment that she truly began to pull free of the Mechanics and her belief in the cogs—one still nestled deep in her pocket, her last token of faith. Freed, not by her own loss, not by meeting the eyes of the Bartender or learning his name, but by seeing others act as she had, only so very, profoundly differently to her, and yet just as certain that they were right. That their way was perfect and beautiful and the only thing worth living for.

The Regular did not, as she stepped into the corridor, take in the exquisite extremes of the building. She had no time for gaudy excesses or the excess of abnegation. She walked with purpose, still burning fresh inside her, the taste of the liquor still on her lips and tongue. She wondered if she should have brought the bottle.

Truth be told, the Bartender would not have sold it to her, for to find purpose inside a bottle and only within its dark golden, honeyed taste, was not the same as finding purpose in action. To find one's purpose in the insides of a bottle was the risk of an excess altogether different. A dangerous path many in the city walked, but none of those who did ever found themselves in *Moderation*.

The Regular let her feet carry her, trusted them like she always did. When she had been little and bloody, they had taken her to the Mechanics, and every day since they had walked her to her station and to her rooms, knowing her place in the world with sure perfection. Today, her feet had not walked her off a tower or a bridge, had not walked her to an alchemist's shop, but they had walked her to *Moderation*, the only place she could have true solace from her pain. So, with no idea what else to do to find her mark, the Regular let her feet walk her where they willed.

Up stairs and along infinite corridors, down more stairs that somehow never seemed to send her back to where she had started, instead the space itself twisting and shifting to please its mood as she walked the halls. She passed many, many doors. At first, she counted and glanced at them, but soon she had lost count and interest both, the muffled noises coming from behind no longer of interest. She had wondered at first, what the murmurs and gasps and groans and moans were all about. She had been tempted to peek inside. But at the last second, hand resting on the handle, she had remembered the Bartender's words.

Open no door until you are sure that is where you want to be.

After a few moments, the repeating noises had lost their mystery and allure and she had simply ploughed on, waiting for that feeling of rightness to wash over her, for that moment when she would know that she was where she was meant to be and her feet would stop of their own accord.

FIVE

Smoke and mirrors, candle flames and dazzling jewels. A glittering heaven bathed in music and laughter and the sounds of people coming together. It was a temple, a place of worship where worshipping meant a never-ending party that spiralled endlessly. It was a temple to beauty. To pleasure. A temple that had found its divinity, its god, its Idol, in a young man with blond curls like the angels of old; in a young man, lost and sorrowful, seeking forgetfulness in a city where the crime that had seen him banished was no crime at all.

The Idol lounged on a throne at the back of the hall, overseeing the festivities from his dais, body loose and languid, clothes draping in sheer layers like folded wings of lace. His green eyes were bright but hooded as though he was lost in a half-dream, his lips parted in what some would have seen as wanton abandon. The Idol was beautiful, his face decorated in curling golden paint, his eyes in hues of greens and blues and his lips in dark, striking red. His hair sat loose, longer now than it had been when Cornucopia had stolen his soul, threaded with rubies and sapphires, turquoises and amethysts.

Clouds of incense wreathed him in shifting mystery, and in them he found the forgetfulness he had sought, the balm for a heart that bled still. The Idol knew it, knew he felt pain deep inside him in the rare, quiet moments where he was left alone. But the story of that pain, the reason behind the ache that seized his chest like a death grip, had been shrouded, entombed so far in the cavernous depth of mind and soul that the Idol could no longer reach it. It was a pain as mysterious to him as he was to his faithful, an unattainable thing dangled within sight but too far to grasp.

In the hall, vast as it was loud, an impossible room in an impossible building, the Idol forgot about the pain as he forgot who he had been before. He forgot that words such as choice had once been his to wield and use. He forgot that there was a world outside of smoke and jewels and dazzling chandeliers. A world outside of walls painted in exquisite renditions of the beautiful, made godly with cleverly painted light. He forgot a world where everything had been forbidden, a world that had left him broken and ready to fall into the waiting arms of worshippers who could tell him all the words he had never heard before.

The Idol watched the crowd, catching eyes burning with desire when they looked at him, gliding over bodies hardly more covered than his own as they laughed and danced and feasted upon food and one another, barely tucked away in curtained alcoves, sprawling on beds of silky cushions, their corners embellished with bells that rang in time with the dance of intertwined bodies.

There were no dark colours within the hall — not that the Idol did not like them, but they brought a twinge of something too much like homesickness. His worshippers had noticed and bright, gaudy cloth had become their attire of choice. They lit a hundred candles to banish shadows that made the Idol's mouth fall into a line, brow creasing in a way that threatened to dislodge the jewel at his forehead.

There was music, always music, to banish the name that the Idol called in his sleep like a prayer, for there could be no-one a divinity called to, no-one a divinity could need in the way the Idol needed the one whose name he called. The one he forgot when he awoke to incense smoke and dizzying touches. To be bathed and dressed and worshipped, to have food brought to his lips when his own limbs felt heavy from the smoke.

Time was a stranger to the Idol, an acquaintance left at the doors of his new home, this impossible world where day and night had long since stopped existing and the only purpose was the worship of beauty and pleasure, of beauty and the flesh. The Idol had forgotten that time had ever been a part of his life, lulling him into routine: a year to frame months and weeks, days to control hours, minutes and seconds to explain all the in-between, all the moments too short and yet so bright. Time was barred entry in a hall with neither windows nor clocks. Here time was only measured in the lull between meals and the length of kisses trailing on skin.

Debauchery.

That was what people in the Idol's past would have called this. A den of iniquity. They would have spoken the words with grimaces on their faces, hands covering mouths, either to feign shock or mimic disgust. They would have hated everything about the hall. About the building it was in. About this city and its people. Even those with lifestyles closer to theirs in their abnegation would have still been sinners for choosing to remain in this place.

Perhaps it was why the Idol had come here.

Perhaps it was why he had willingly fallen into the arms of worshippers.

Perhaps...

The Idol did not remember now, more memories turned to smoke and ash and locked away. The Idol did not want to remember, did not want to think of the before.

But always something inside him felt ready to wake, like another set of eyes wanting to open within his heart. Eyes who knew where the cave in his soul hid. Eyes he was content to keep closed. Eyes he wanted to blind with smoke and burning touches, drowning them in his newfound status.

The Idol stood forever at the crossroad of memory and abandon, only partially aware where his steps took him. Memories were hard things to discard when one wanted to, and so easy to misplace when one needed them. How easy to forget a cherished voice, or a lesson one wished to keep in mind, but how hard to banish bruising hands, spilt blood, and fear.

The Idol stood in one fluid motion, the cape of gauze and lace falling away from him. The hall fell quiet, all eyes turning to him. He saw them kneel, watched their beautiful faces and knew he would find relief in one of them. Never for long, certainly not once the deed was done, but enough to take his mind away from the sudden surge of terror that washed over him unannounced and unwelcomed. Graceful step by graceful step, he came down from the dais, the silk of his wide pants whispering a song even above the music.

He looked at faces, seeking something he did not recognise. He reached out to some but never touched, unsure of his choice even as so many eyes roamed over him, pleading to be blessed by his touch.

Time walked into the room.

Though to say it walked would be incorrect. Time, after all, has no legs with which to carry itself. And although this particular incarnation of time—a small watch on a dull bronze chain tucked in a pocket full of memories in the form of tickets and receipts—belonged to someone who had legs, the Stranger did not use them to enter the hall. It would be more correct to say that time wheeled itself into the room, with hardly more than a whisper and the creaking of spokes. It should have been no big event at all, just another body adding itself to the ones already inside, too many for the Idol to keep count.

But the Stranger did not belong within the hall, with his dark clothes and his timepiece. With his face free of adornments and the grim set of his jaw.

He was like a rock dropped into a pond, sending ripples coursing through the surface of worshippers as they went from staring at the Idol, to staring at him. The Idol too, lifted his heavily made-up eyes to look at this new and unexpected arrival, this interruption to his existence, so forceful in its quiet, unassuming nature. A flash like lightning ran through him as his eyes met the Stranger's, as though the crossroad he stood at had been struck and was crumbling away.

The Stranger froze in place, not because of the hundred faces suddenly turned to him, but because of the green eyes that met his own blue ones. Green eyes full of something that was not quite recognition and not quite fear. Green eyes that burned with something not quite right although not so wrong as to be noticeable. A difference only the Stranger could have seen. A difference the Idol felt in everything he did.

'Tick' went the timepiece and although it had not quite been a sound, only a movement hidden by fabric and pocket and the arm of the wheelchair, the crowd of worshippers reacted at once. They stood, a wave of bodies barring the Idol from the Stranger, keeping the Stranger from the Idol. A wave of bodies that surrounded the Idol so swiftly that he felt dizzy. He did not see the Stranger backing out of the room, eyes wide with fear, heart racing with dread. He did not see the way the crowd pushed him back or the girl walking down the corridor, her feet waiting to find purchase on the purpose she had been promised.

The Idol saw nothing but bodies.

And then a hand on his chest, soft and gentle and warm. A blink and the feel of time was gone, the crossroad back intact as the incense smoke wafted over him. Another hand, on his back this time, as they whispered their apologies for the interruptions, promised they did not understand how one so unworthy had managed to find his way to their sacred hall. They whispered in his ears, whispered as their lips brushed his neck and collarbones, all the time asking for more, begging for the blessing of permission.

The Idol almost said no. Almost pushed them all away, the clarity of those blue eyes still burning through him.

More incense smoke washed over him, a glass of water touched his lips and he found he was parched. After that there was no thought of refusal, no desire to embrace the knowledge that the entrance of time in his domain had been a call to memory, a call to himself. He closed his eyes as he wrapped his arms around a boy with golden brown skin and hair darker than night itself. The kiss came next, not tentative or hesitant, but deep and passionate. Other hands became lost in his hair, touching his back, touching him.

The Idol threw his head back as they whispered their prayers to him, and he let them worship him. But behind his closed lids, he saw not the hall, not the gilded lights and bright fabric, but an austere hall and a boy with neat black hair and serious blue eyes. A boy in a wheelchair.

A Stranger whose name had always been the prayer on the Idol's lips.

SIX

ending a bar was an endless affair of pouring drinks and cleaning glasses, polishing smears and wiping stains. It was the tedium of waxing wood and righting fallen chairs when card games went south, and tempers took people outside of *Moderation*. The cards he left scattered: an ace tucked against the wall, a queen fallen on a chair, and a three stuck upright in between floorboards. Their owners would return to claim back the deck. And if they did not, their opponent probably would. He knew the cards would not stay there for long. They never did.

Moderation was as quiet as it ever got, only three lone souls at its tables, all separate and wreathed in their own silent thoughts, nursing three different drinks in three, equally different glasses. There was a black liquid in a glass like a stylised heart, a steaming green one in a bowl like an upside down tree canopy, and finally a clear one, in a clear glass, the two merging so perfectly that it was hard to tell where glass ended and liquid began. He had poured each drink with the same careful consideration, and now his patrons drank and faced the truth of what they had come asking for.

The Bartender wondered what had become of the Stranger, and of the Regular he had sent after him. There was darkness in the Stranger's heart. Unheard pain. A sense of loss that spoke not only of losing something outside oneself but something inside. A detachment. A loss of roots. In that, he was much like the Regular, only her freshly plucked roots bled still whilst his had hardened into a permanent frown and the severe line of his mouth. It had been a slow uprooting, as though he had grown half out of the soil that should have been his.

A glass set back on the shelf, another picked up. A pause then, as a man walked in. He did not look at the Bartender and the Bartender did not look at him as he retrieved his cards. There was a bruise on his cheek and anger in his eyes.

"You should stay in," the Bartender said, and although he wasn't looking at the man, it was obvious who he was speaking to. "There are bad things on the streets, and too many fights waiting for a spark."

The man whirled, though his body language was more startled than menacing.

"What if I want a fight?"

The Bartender shrugged. This man was not his responsibility, not outside *Moderation*. And yet he was here now, a pack of cards in one hand, a knife tucked at his back. He was here, and the Bartender understood too well the ways of the city.

"I wouldn't mind a game of cards," the Bartender said, setting down one glass for another, discarding a dirty cloth for a clean one. "It's quiet and I'm almost out of glasses to clean."

This was not the first time the Bartender had had this very conversation. Not with this man, no, but with others like him, full of anger and carved into sharp angles as ready to cut as they were to break. This was a well-practised dance where he was partner and hunter, his patron the prey unwittingly waltzing to his tune. The cards were simply the lure. And, just as the Bartender had expected, it had drawn the man in.

"Cards? Never seen you playin' cards before," the man retorted. His accent was thick. Once a stranger to Cornucopia but now just another face, another lost soul.

The Bartender did not know his excess or abnegation, did not know if he worshipped. His clothes did not give him away and, either way, it was of little import.

"I don't like doing nothing," the Bartender replied.

And like that, the man was at the bar, the cards moving fast in his hand as he shuffled them. The Bartender reached for a liquor that matched the man's shirt and poured a small glass of it, setting it down at his side.

"On the house," he said.

There, the hint of a smile, the power of a kindness. The cards were dealt. The Bartender picked up two Jacks and a Queen. He thought of the Stranger and the Regular and the boy they searched for. He glanced out of the window as the patron hummed, and although he could not see the Cathedral of Idols from where he stood, the Bartender felt the presence of those he had sent out into the city all the same.

SEVEN

The Stranger felt sick. Down to his bones. The door slammed shut, faces pressing to the glass pane, warped and distorted as he tried to remember how to breathe, how to think. All he could do was shake; his mind still fixed on the bright green eyes that had met his own. Eyes bright with fever and drugs and all the things he had been afraid of. Bright with forgetting. Because of course he had come here to forget. What other reasons would he have had to come here apart from to wipe his slate clean? To start again. Well woven lies had sent him away and the Stranger had not had the chance to speak. And now he'd had no time to call the Idol's name and speak his truth. Or perhaps it would be more correct to say that there had been time for such admissions, but the Stranger had frozen. In that room outside of time he had forgotten how to exist, how to move and speak and be. In that room outside of time, he had become unravelled in bright green eyes, like he had done before in a room where time most definitely existed, and the ticking of the clock had kept them from foolish acts.

The Stranger did not know what he felt. He would have liked to say nothing, that those green eyes had not pierced right through to his soul like an arrow and left behind a trail of blood in the shape of tears. But there were tears, silent and wet down his cheeks, and there was pain, with no blood to mark it, no wound to translate how he felt inside.

He had succeeded and failed in the same breath. Found and lost again.

What was he to do against a room full of people ready to worship, to protect, to keep him away from the only person he wanted near? He should have asked the Bartender more questions, but as is often the case in such endeavours, he knew only now what questions he might have asked, what answers were needed.

"You look lost."

When the Stranger opened his eyes, he saw only a pair of feet. He looked up, slowly discovering a woman around his age with dark brown skin and darker hair, with clothing he had not seen around this part of the city. She looked about as out of place as he did, neither part of abnegation or excess, her clothing sensible though he could see the places where patches had been roughly removed, leaving behind only traces of what had been before, a handful of threads that lead only to loss and sorrow.

"So do you," he responded, though that wasn't true. There had been something final and purposeful about the way she had stopped in front of him. As though she, unlike him, had meant to be here

"I was. Until I found you."

The Stranger blinked, unsure who she was or why she would be looking for him. She had a striking face, the kind he would like to stop and draw, so he knew he would have remembered her. He had passed many faces on his way through Cornucopia, but he was quite confused as to why anyone would have been seeking him out. He was a stranger after all, and few were those who actively sought out those such as he unless it was for some more nefarious deed than she looked to be here for. Her posture was guarded, speaking of pain, and his eyes once again drifted to the myriad of little threads that outlined the absence of something.

"You were looking for me?"

"The Bartender sent me," she answered simply.

The Stranger relaxed at her openness even though her expression did not change, relaxed at the knowledge that the man who had guided his feet here in the first place had sent someone to... But to what? Help? Hinder? Guide? He had no idea. After all, there would have been no way for the Bartender to know what he would find behind the door, no way for him to know that the Stranger would find himself lost and stranded.

"Why?" He thought it wiser to ask, rather than assume, especially in a city he understood so little about. What did the girl worship, what *thing* was hers to believe in truly, fully? And would knowing that give him any inkling as to what she was like? The Stranger came from a city where worshipping anything but the one Entity was a crime punished severely. He did not understand the freedom of Cornucopia, had thought upon hearing about it that it would be true freedom, to choose your own faith, your own idol.

But in that too, Cornucopia was an excess. Too much of a good thing, after all, turned the good right back to bad, like an hourglass spinning back around once it was spent of every grain.

"He didn't say. Said you needed finding, that you might become lost looking for someone else. And he wanted me to find you before you could no longer be found."

The Stranger shook his head. From behind the door he could hear sounds that turned his stomach. The sounds of people coming together. The sounds of a joy bought at the price of one's sanity, of a happiness clouded in smoke to dull the mind and craze the senses. Anger rose to replace the upset, to mask it, a clumsy bandage for the depth of the wound. But the Stranger had precious else left to use. He wanted a drink. Or maybe ten. He wanted *home*, though he had never known a *home* worthy of that title. Not when the place he should have been able to call so had been dark and cold and cruel, shaped by a man who had matched his surroundings well and a woman whose heart had turned to stone long before he had been born.

"I found him," he whispered softly, an admission like spitting thorns.

"And?"

"I cannot reach him."

"Why not?"

The Stranger thought back to the impossible room and the people there, all dressed in such bright, provocative clothes, their eyes heavy with paint and their hands hungry for one another. The Stranger thought of how *wrong* the hall had felt, how he had known without needing to ask or be told that he did not belong there. His clothing was dark as the expression in his eyes, an offence to that place. He did not mean to tell the woman what he had seen in the hall, but he did. Not in great detail, for he could not wax lyrical with words as he might have been able to with a pencil on paper, but he told her nonetheless. Of the Idol whom he sought and the Worshippers that stood in his way. He did not describe the room in the details of poets and writers, but with the brevity of a man who had seen more than he knew how to handle. He did not cry as he spoke, though tears danced in his eyes like so much rain waiting to fall, and the woman said nothing, arms crossed against her chest as she stood, waiting for him to be done. At last he was finished, and silence fell over them, enveloping not like a blanket, warm and comforting, but like a sack pulled over one's head, suffocating and threatening.

"I think we should go back to *Moderation*," the woman said after only a moment's pause. "The Bartender might know something that can help."

She did not wait to see if the Stranger would follow, simply turning on her heels and heading back down the path she had come from.

EIGHT

The Regular found that she was rather eager to be out of the unfamiliar corridors. The tale the Stranger had woven for her had chilled her to the bone. A room full of madmen, minds addled by drugs, their routine one of chaos and brightness and mess. All things she could not imagine. All things she had never wanted. At least there had been no blood, no knife to cut and scar, no white marble to stain. At least there had been sound instead of eerie silence.

The Stranger was quiet save for the creaking of his wheels. The corridors stretched on endlessly and after a while he let out a groan of frustration as he was forced to ask for a break. She wondered how long they had walked for. Longer, it seemed, than she had when first coming in. Her feet were not being reliable in leading her back out. Quite the contrary it seemed, and the Stranger was as lost as she. They came to a stop at the top of stairs that caused the Stranger's forehead to draw into a V.

"There were no stairs when I came," he noted. "We must be going the wrong way."

"I came up too many stairs to count when I came to find you," the Regular replied, her expression now matching the Stranger's. His frustration was palpable as he looked from the chair to the stairs, to the corridor behind them.

It wasn't as though they'd had any choice on which way to go. The corridor had offered no branching path, only one single way winding and curling inside the impossible building. The Regular turned back to look at the stairs, then back again at the corridor. She could have sworn it had changed, shifting almost under her very gaze. The doors seemed more numerous now, each numbered and from behind them a rhythmic noise that could almost have been music.

Chik chik cha chik chika cha ding ziiiiip

Over and over again, a hundred typewriters, typing. Typing. *Typing.* Until the sound was dizzying. Until it mounted and mounted, and the world felt as though it would slip out from under her feet. She could barely see the Stranger at her side, his hands clamped over his ears as though that would do anything to protect him from the racket.

Chik chik chik cha cha chik chika chik ding ziiiiip

The Regular gasped. It was hard to breathe. Harder to stand. The ground came to meet her knees as the typewriters built to a crescendo and then, as suddenly as it had come, the sound was gone. It rang in the aftermath, left ears tingling and senses dulled. Neither spoke for a long while, catching their breath. The Regular did not understand how the Temple of Idols worked, how its many rooms could coexist within the building, for although it was large, she knew it was not large enough. Not so that it never ran out of space no matter how many new Idols came to town, no matter how many new people joined a cult.

"What was that?" the Stranger asked, his voice strained with fear.

"I don't know," the Regular admitted. "There are so many idols registered no-one can hope to keep track of them all and of what their followers do. But..."

She turned back to the corridor. It had shifted again. This time it was bathed in deep crimson light, each door carved to resemble some monstrous face. The Regular had to swallow the urge to scream, swallow it with her fear. There was wicked laughter from behind the doors, echoing over and over again, like a reflection caught in between two mirrors, endlessly repeating itself. She turned away, and met the gaunt, terrified face of her companion. Had the Bartender known this would happen if she came or was that something even he could not foresee?

"I think it's trying to find where we belong," she told the Stranger, voice shaking.

The laughter had not yet died down, and where the typewriters had made her feel dizzy, this was making her feel sick. The Stranger looked frightened and she could see his determination cracking behind his eyes. There were things, inexplicable things, woven into the fabric of Cornucopia, and strangers were rarely prepared for them. The real question lay in whether she could face them or not. This, painted in red and screams, was her past. Her past of clean white dresses and blood-stained blades. But her past was also greasy hands and tidy cogs, stained leathers and heavy goggles.

She only needed to decide what her present held. What her future promised.

"I think I know how to get out of here. But we're going to have to be quick," she said, pulling herself up against the fear and the laughter.

"I can't—" the Stranger started, motioning at the chair, but she was behind him already.

"Can I?"

He only hesitated for a breath. "Yes."

She took off through the red-tinged corridor, pushing the Stranger before her. There was a knife on the floor he called for her to avoid and they swayed. Her eyes closed against the fear until he shouted at her before she could hit a wall. She stopped, a breathless apology on her lips. And then she opened her eyes.

Gone were the red lights. Gone was the laughter. The typewriters were nothing but the memory of a nightmare. Instead they stood in front of an ebony door with glass panels and gold letters painted elegantly onto its surface.

EXIT.

With shaking hands, the Regular pushed it open. It took some work, the door rusty and rarely used, but at last the two of them were out in what passed for fresh air in Cornucopia. The Stranger let out a noise that was half sob, half hysterical laughter, but all the Regular could do was stand there, shaking faintly.

"What happened?" The Stranger asked when he had regained control of his breathing.

"Some things are best left unexplained," she said, but her voice carried her grief, her pain, like a bag weighing heavy on her back, dragging her down, down, down. She had grown so accustomed to its presence that she thought she had dropped it. "Let's go, I don't think we should go back in there until we have a plan."

The Regular did not see the way the Stranger looked up sharply as her use of 'we'. She did not see, in his brilliant blue eyes, the tears brought along by an unearned kindness, by an offer of companionship that he had not known in far too long. The Regular did not see, and so she did not realise her own power. Born not of cogs and order, or of blood and chanted words. Simpler, yet more complicated than any power Cornucopia had ever granted her.

NINE

The Bartender glanced at them from the corner of his eye, wet and dishevelled, hands cupped around mugs of hot tea in place of alcohol, something he had deemed better and deposited wordlessly at their table. It had started to rain about an hour ago, somewhere in between them leaving the Cathedral of Idols and returning to *Moderation*, and it had not spared them. The Bartender understood rain was not keen on sparing anyone, but he thought that for once it might have been decent of it to hold itself back long enough to see two lost, shaken innocents find safety. Instead it seemed keen on soaking the Stranger at every chance.

It was raining still, battering the windows and soaking the floor by the front door every time someone came in. If it carried on, the Bartender thought he might be in for a lot of mopping. It made for boring work, but it was sometimes a refreshing change from polishing glasses. There was something soothing about the back-forth-lift-wring out rhythm. There was a music to it, like there was a music to glasses setting down on tables and being refilled, or to the motions of fingers in the air.

And then there was the less pleasant music of fingernails on wood. *Tap. Tap. Tap.* Like an aggressive faucet not shut properly. *Tap. Tap. Tap.* The sound of frustration. *Tap. Tap. Tap.*

The Bartender whirled to the Regular as her fingers completed another loop of the rhythm. Her eyes were lost in her untouched cup—he should be offended; it was his best tea for warming the soul—her hand moving of its own accord. At her side, the Stranger was drinking his tea, it seemed, to do something. There were tears in his eyes, brightening their blue to almost unnatural degrees. But he too looked as though he had seen ghosts, though his, the Bartender guessed, were of the future and not the past.

Part of him considered not getting involved. He had offered answers and granted purpose and that, really, was more than he would have done on most days. But there was something about the Stranger's stunning blue eyes and the Regular's unshed tears that struck a chord inside him. Both were victims of this city, and although the Bartender would never admit to it, there were many who suspected *Moderation* was the only safety from the madness and contagion of Cornucopia. Those that did not whisper that his eyes held madness spoke instead of how the bar was the only place they could think, the unceasing movement of his hands directing their thoughts much in the way a conductor led an orchestra.

He glanced to his shelves—neat and clean and arranged—and pursed his lips in thought. There was no single answer to this question, instead many solutions presented themselves, leaving him wondering which he ought to choose. His fingers danced from one bottle to the next, caressing a tall one of golden liquid before jumping to a curling cylinder of azure. Each had a name, and each had a story, and only he knew them. Only he needed to. Few were those who came to *Moderation* and asked for a particular drink, though he kept beer, whiskey, and the like for such people. Most came with a problem, a question, a wound, a tale to tell but no words to tell it with. And he found them drinks that answered or gifted words or cleared their mind. He found them drinks that gave purpose or courage or a new outlook on life. He found them drinks that dulled hatred of the self, and those that painted the worlds in soothing pastel shades when every colour was an edge sharp as a knife to too-keen senses.

None needed to know the names of what they drank. Truly, none wanted to. Sometimes to know a thing's name is to take away its magic, its power. And no-one, least of all the Bartender, wanted these bottles and their contents to lose their powers. To the Regular and the Stranger he could give forgetfulness or the urge to travel, he could give crimson liquor to replace a missing heart, or one the colour of fog that would dull all their pain for the rest of their lives at the price of their soul—he had only poured it once for a man who had outlived too many, and had only revenge left as family. It had not been an easy decision, to watch pain fade alongside a soul, but the Bartender had known the lives that would be saved. He had never seen the man again.

At last he made his choice, a dark bottle the colour of ink that promised an exquisite shade of sapphire when poured. The Bartender selected two glasses, neither too plain, but plain enough that the colour of the drink would not turn the vessel into jewel instead of glass. He deposited the glasses in front of his patrons and poured each of them a drink. He did not meet their eyes, but they both could easily tell that his attention was on them, pressing if not insistent. When neither moved, he sighed at their stubbornness.

"Drink," he said, standing by the side of their table, waiting.

"What will it do?" The Regular asked, because she knew more than most that when the Bartender himself brought you a drink, there was always a reason behind it. The Stranger hesitated with it halfway to his lips.

"It will help," the Bartender replied simply.

The Regular eyed him suspiciously but the Stranger was desperate for any help—never a good position to find oneself in—and downed the small glass in one. The Bartender allowed a smile to play on his lips as the Regular looked from him to the Stranger for a few seconds before following suit. He glanced behind him, at the table playing cards and the lone woman in the side alcove, and, having ascertained that all was well, he turned back to his two guests.

"So," he started, settling down in a chair across from them. A chair that might as well have appeared out of thin air. "I suppose you should tell me what happened."

TEN

There were three doors in the Idol's chamber. One painted like a vision of the sea and leading onto his bathing chamber, another grand, golden, and gaudy, and leading to the hall. Then there was the third. It was small, narrower than most doors though no shorter, its handle plain black and round, looking as though it would be the perfect size for his hand to fit around. Only the Idol's hand had never closed on it, his fingers had never so much as brushed against the plain wood. It was a door of no interest. Too plain. Too ugly. Too dark, as though it held monsters caged in blackwood and ebony. Neither his eyes nor his hands strayed to the door, not even a wandering thought snagged on it.

There had been no need, in truth, his world wrapped carefully from silk bed to bathing chamber to the glittering hall beyond. Only these places existed and only these places mattered, the chaos of an unpredictable routine stealing thoughts and desires beyond those of the flesh.

Only today had been different.

Today there had been an interruption, something to mark this day against all the others. Today was a *day*. It had detached itself from the formless flow of time that had ensnared him since he had been brought here, clad in silks and jewels. There had been days then. A unit of time marked at their very core by the *tik, tok, tik, tok,* of seconds. Seconds that made minutes that made hours that made, eventually, days. *Tik, tok,* like the watch in the pocket of the Stranger with bright blue eyes.

Tik, tok, like the grandfather clock in his father's mahogany office.

The Idol blinked. He had not thought of his father in a long time. Only he did not know how long for, as time was almost a stranger to him now. But once... Once, it had not been. Once time had marked his days like bathing and eating and touching now did. Had it been better? The Idol did not know. He felt lost, swimming within his own mind, his senses distant from the lips still gracing his collarbones and the hands washing him clean.

He did not remember getting into the giant bath that was his own, though now he felt the petals against his skin, bobbing by and then gone again. He had always liked the petals, liked how they clung to him, so many red blooms like painless blood. *He* was blooming amongst them. A proof of his beauty, his worth. The incense made him heady, drowned thoughts as surely as the water would have taken him if firm hands had not stopped him from slipping under. He didn't mean to, but it was so hard to keep himself grounded.

There were words all around him, but he did not hear them, only the echo of a murmur as his eyes closed, even though they had been shut already. Layers of darkness enveloped him. Darkness of abandon, and darkness of forgetting. The darkness of the incense and the darkness of exhaustion following what had transpired in the hall.

Tik, tok.

The timepiece had barely been audible over the creak of spokes, but it was embedded in his head, so firmly stuck that none of his efforts could dislodge it. It pulled at him painfully, tugging on some invisible rope as it dragged him down, down, down, to memory and pain, to the burning ground he never wanted to touch again. There was so much good, floating high up in the sky, lost to the lesser world below.

Tik, tok.

A melody that grated as hands washed him. There were scents in his hair to excite his senses, but his senses had taken leave, pushing, pulling, tugging. *Seeking*. In his gaze, the Idol did not understand what they sought. He wished to seek nothing, to exist only in this place, in this moment.

Until today.

Until time had *tik, tok*'ed its way in and shattered the illusion. Nothing that had come after had made the Idol blind to it, nothing enough to make him forget the sound of the pocket-watch and the bright blue eyes that had stared right at him. Right into his soul. Blue eyes deeper than the sea painted on his door, brighter than any sapphire to have hung from his throat, more heart-stopping than any jewel. Blue eyes that spoke of a time before. *Before*. Before gilded make-up and hands upon hands on his skin and the chant of his worshippers. A time before incense baths and timeless days spent in only half-awareness.

Tik.

Tok.

His eyes snapped open, as though seeing for the very first time. The water around him was milky and he wondered if it had ever been water at all, the petals floating on its surface like so many drops of blood on a marble floor. A hand flew to his nose, memories overlapping reality, and whoever was there washing him gasped at his sudden motion. The Idol blinked, tearing his gaze away from the bloody petals.

"Out," he croaked. "Out!" His voice found strength.

He had pulled himself upright, standing up to his waist in his milky bath, his heart racing even as he heard murmurs of worry behind him.

"I said, out," he quieted his voice. Tried to remember who he was to them and how to comport himself.

He was probably just tired. He needed rest. Yes, rest would quiet the *tik tok* and the blood-on-marble floor. Resting would dull the blue eyes still burning in his mind.

They protested, his worshippers, though their words felt like an incomprehensible jumble as more incense smoke wafted his way. He staggered, pulling away from the hands reaching out for him. Suddenly words lay forgotten, scattered and broken and sinking, sinking, sinking, so far away from him. Thoughts followed them, his mouth thick, thirst suddenly clawing at his throat as his knees grew weak and weaker still.

Tik.

Tok.

The Idol was aware then, that something was very, very wrong. In the deafening silence of his reeling mind broken only by the splashing of someone joining him in the bath, he was aware of himself for the first time in so very long. He saw through the eyes of memories the city as he had first seen it, bathed in smog and rain, threatening and fascinating.

It had been everything he had feared. Everything he had wanted. He saw the twisting metal spires and the grand stone buildings impossible in their size and grandeur, all the more so when contrasted with the small, dilapidated houses scattered about them.

There was a hand on his wrist, though he could not tell if that was now, or then. He was lost, as trapped within the memory as he was in his chambers. The incense calmed the heart that wanted to race, silenced the scream his mouth shaped. The world spun. He was lost. Had been lost. Even before he had arrived in Cornucopia. He had been lost for so long he was not sure he could ever be found again. Water sloshed; rain fell. There was laughter and screams and the leftovers of a feast. A hotel of gilded columns and grand archways, with shackles by the beds.

His body lolled in the grasp of his captor, though he did not know when he was being carried. He remembered running, but there would be no running now, his legs but two dead weights too heavy for him to lift. Even his head was only weight. He remembered a man with the look of someone who understood this city. Eyes of coal. Like his soul. He remembered questions and a smile that had been that of a predator. Had he been a keen prey? Had he fought?

Would he fight?

When was he? *Where* was he?

Soft silks under him, a pillow under his head. Worried murmurs asking if it was 'too much' mingling with the reassurance that he just needed rest. A man with eyes like coal had promised him a place to belong. A place where all his desires would be answered. But what had been the price? He could not remember. He could hardly conjure up more than the man's eyes as the silks cooled his body.

What was happening to him?

Everything had been fine; everything had been right before the blue eyes and the pocket-watch and the *tik tok* of memory. He was unravelling, bits of himself scattering like so many leaves on the wind of change. The whispers around him were dying down. Rest, yes, they would let him rest and so they would rest too, for everything in the hall was dictated by whatever rhythm he chose. Or was it? Was it his choice to rest now? Had any of it been his choice?

The Idol blinked, his thoughts more jumbled than his sheets, forcing his eyes to open. The canopy of silks and gauze came into focus, bright colours almost too much to bear. Slowly, very slowly, he shifted, rolled onto his side. He was naked still, and aware of his body in a way that reminded him that the incense still burned. His eyes did not look for the burner though, going instead to the ebony door. The narrow door and all the questions he had never asked. Slowly, so very slowly, the Idol pulled himself off the bed. He could not stand, legs too weak and head too light, so he dragged himself on hands and knees, until at last he was in front of the door.

But before his hand could find the handle, blackness washed over him.

ELEVEN

I t was a tale as old as Cornucopia.

As old as a city made on unkept promises. As old as the world itself, for there had always been those whose parents, families, societies, did not know how to accept. Those that were branded sinners, liars, tainted, demonic, or simply wrong for the shape of their soul. Souls that loved and wept and felt in all the ways that were right for them but wrong for the world that refused to make space for what was different.

It was a tale of friendship and love, of dangerous kisses shared in the dark. A tale of love shattered by those who did not understand it. Who did not want to try. Whose own love had been dictated for them, their very lives only a repetition of what had come before. Hatred repeated with no context, ideas of right and wrong forged in a time long gone. It was a tale of heartbreak and anger and pain. Of promises broken and of hopes shattered. But it was also a tale of courage, of heads held high against a storm. Of tear-stained letters that never ceased to believe that love was right. That love would win.

Until love had been sent away.

And then it became a chase, a tale of adventure, against the odds. Against the world. Against *everything*.

The bones of the tale were simple as a child's drawing, two lines for two boys in love in a world where their love was severely punished. One sent away, the other imprisoned at home. Until the day when the prisoner boy had found a way to escape and come searching for the boy who had been sent away.

Cornucopia had not been his first stop after leaving Faith—his home city, one whose name made the Bartender shudder—but now here he was, months down the line, a little older and a lot wiser, yet with blue eyes not filled with harsh steel but with the tears of a broken heart, of hope wilting under a too-hot sun.

The tea was gone, and so was the liquor of powdered sapphire, leaving behind only silence. The lone woman had finished her tall glass of sunset and gone on her way, to search for the moment she had drank and the arms of the one who waited for her there. The men at the card table had ended their game with laughter instead of a knife, leaving together arm in arm, their old, bearded faces bearing grins that had not been theirs to wear in a long time. *Moderation* was quiet now, only the Stranger, the Regular, and the Bartender remaining, silent as three statues as they contemplated the truths laid bare in front of them like poker players studying their cards.

The Bartender's butterfly hands played a silent melody on the table, nails and fingertips never quite meeting the surface. It was also a game, to see how close he could get without making a sound. A game he had long since mastered, the way he had mastered humming tunes so that no-one but him could hear. A game, like everything in life, really, just a set of rules and an end goal. Sometimes well defined, sometimes not, all depending on what board you had been gifted: was it old and dusted, having passed through so many hands that the words were almost impossible to read? Or was it new and shiny, truly your own to follow, the rules crisply written black on white or white on black?

"I don't know what to do. I... I don't think he recognised me."

Those were the first words spoken in *Moderation* for close to a quarter of an hour, fifteen long minutes that could have been fifteen seconds or fifteen hours. Fifteen seconds to the Bartender creating a melody, his mind already weaving the ending to a song of tragic love, and fifteen hours to the Stranger, lost in his grief and sorrow. Perhaps the truest arbiter of time was the Regular, eyes hard, one hand a fist, one endlessly tracing the rim of her glass in a rhythm only the Bartender noticed.

One rotation for every ten seconds, ninety rotation since the last words the Bartender had spoken.

What will you do?

That had been his question. It was meant to have a simple answer, one of a pair: *I will find a way* or *He is lost to me*, but it was clear that the Stranger had taken the question as more demanding, requiring thought and a plan, as though he alone could achieve it all, as though he did not require help to make it all reality. It told the Bartender things, spoke to him of a lonely heart that struggled to slot himself within the world, of a hurting soul upon whom so many expectations had been placed that no creature, not even immortal, could have possibly fulfilled all of them to any degree of satisfaction.

"Will you leave, then?" the Bartender asked, his eyes tracing patterns into the wooden pillar to the left of the Stranger's head.

He did not need to look upon his face to know the frown that twisted his brow.

"Of course not. I only meant that..." he faltered.

Admitting truths was always hard, but always so necessary if one were to move past what held them back.

The Regular looked to the Stranger, whose own eyes were very far away. His eyes were sad and hers were steel, and for a moment the Bartender considered leaving them alone. They would be fine, he thought. His love and sorrow would temper her steel whilst she sharpened him and together, together they could do this.

But then both sets of eyes—sorrow and steel and everything in between—came to rest upon him. The Bartender sighed, not a theatrical gesture meant to be heard and noticed. No, his sigh was a tiny thing, an exhale of breath, barely a sound and meant only for himself.

"It is not easy, facing what you have faced," he said to the Stranger, though his eyes were elsewhere, both in their direction and their focus, though none would have known to where they had strayed. "To come this far only to find yourself...*forgotten*. Although, you must ask yourself whether you believe that. Do you truly believe he has forgotten you?"

"I..."

The Bartender interrupted him with a graceful gesture that demanded attention. "If you did not believe the words of your peers and your parents, why would you believe what you saw today?"

The Stranger frowned. "Because I *saw* it. Eyes could not lie as well as his did, not when they were so devoid of anything. I know what I *saw*. How could I not believe it?"

Something like a smile tugged at the corners of the Regular's lips. She made to reach for the bottle of red liquor that had been sitting between them all for the best part of half an hour now, but the bartender touched her hand lightly, barely more than the tips of his finger against her hand—and shook his head. *Not yet*.

"You think your eyes cannot lie to you?" She asked of the Stranger, who looked as though it was the most bizarre thing he had ever been asked. The answer was written in his frown. "Well you're wrong. Here everything can lie to you, and most everyone will want to."

"This is not Mendacity," the Stranger retorted, and the Bartender grimaced at the mention of another of the Fractured Cities, rising like ghosts in the endless wasteland.

"No, but did they not also lie to you in Faith? Of course, they did, to pass on their beliefs. Cornucopia lies to ensnare, to trap you. Mendacity does it because it's its nature." The Bartender told him.

The Stranger chewed his lip, the Bartender could almost read the thoughts in his head, all the fears that hampered his eyes from truly opening.

"I have to go back there, don't I?" he asked, in a voice considerably smaller than he wanted. "I have to go back there, and I have to *really* look. At him, at that place, at everything. And then, then what? Will they just let him go?"

"That, surprisingly, is up to him," the Bartender spoke, his voice soft and stretching out to fill the terrifying moments of silence in between word and heartbeat. "Cornucopia likes to ensnare, yes, but it does not like to keep what does not wish to be kept. It is not a prison, only a rotten jewel built around the dying embers of passion." As he spoke, the Bartender slanted his head towards the Regular, as though whispering something to her. Wordless, and perhaps unneeded, if he judged her longing looks towards the bar correctly.

Perhaps, amid it all, there was still a life for her here.

"I need to at least... I need to try and talk to him. I need to *know*," the Stranger's words were still a little hesitant, but there was something new in his eyes and this time the Bartender did not keep the Regular from grabbing the bottle. She poured herself a shot and poured one to the Stranger. All the while the Bartender was watching her, not the young man whose determination was resurfacing, putting itself back together.

"Do not trust your eyes," the Bartender said. "In the place where you are headed, only your heart can guide you."

The Stranger nodded, fingers a little shaky as they grasped the glass in front of him, the liquor red like fresh blood, red like the heart in which he needed to trust. The Bartender smiled at the pair then and watched, not without curiosity, as the Regular waited to see the Stranger drink before she downed her own shot. It was as though he could see her place within the world shift more with every second, becoming less of *there* and more of *here*. She wasn't fully of the *here* yet, but the *there* was almost fully behind her.

"I will go back. I will find him, and I will not be afraid," the Stranger said, and the words he spoke were true although he was afraid. But often, when people speak of not being afraid, they do not speak of not knowing fear, but of not letting fear rule their actions and their lives. Which was precisely what the Stranger meant.

When he lifted his gaze from his glass to almost meet the Bartender's, the blue in them was sharper, brighter, as though the light that lived inside him had been rekindled with a thought. A hope. A promise and a maybe. There were no guarantees, not even for the Bartender who knew the ways of Cornucopia better than most. But there was a chance. And sometimes, after all, it is the smallest chance, the tiniest hope, that fuels the actions that change the course of history.

"You two should go. Whether you go to rest first or head straight there, this place is about to get busy," the Bartender told them, pushing to his feet. "One thing, before you go," he added as the Regular stood and the Stranger pushed his chair away from the table. "When all is said and done, come for another drink."

He turned from them, then, to the door that opened, a large group of people—easily a dozen—staggering through the doors. Their faces were stained in soot and their clothes spoke of hard work and too little money. They did not seem to notice the eerie way the Bartender appeared back behind the bar, and they did not spare a glance to the odd pair leaving *Moderation*. They were too worn down and trampled, their god demanding always more, always too much. So, the Bartender set about pouring the same drink he had always poured for them, the same drinks to soothe soul and body, and to forget a little more each day why this god of theirs was the only thing that mattered.

In truth, it was not something he should have done, akin to the breaking of a sacred covenant, but the Bartender did not believe in bargains made with bullies, and so he served the drinks, and the people drank and slowly, so very, very slowly, became freer at last.

TWELVE

Some might think that now comes the decisive moment in this story. The realisation of all that has occurred before, the sum of all the parts. But in truth, that had already happened. Not as a grand moment of courage or battle, not as a daring rescue or the taking down of a foe. Those are not the decisive moments of a story, but its inevitable conclusion. There is little decisive about a battle, often won or lost in careful planning or eager recklessness. Often, victory or loss has been decided long before what is seen as the climax, the apex of a story. It happens in quieter moments, those the bards cannot so easily weave into tales to excite the imagination.

No, the true decisive moment is usually nothing more than a look, a word, the straightening of shoulders. It is often an act so small as to be missed that turns the tide. The pouring of a drink, the realisation of one's true capability, the embrace of a friend or ally. Sometimes there is only one such moment, sometimes they come as a multitude. Not battles. Not blood and swords and fighting. Just people, *any* person, whose heart becomes set on the task ahead. There is your decisive moment: in that small, tiny moment, where hesitation gives way to determination, to the belief that one can succeed.

Without that moment, well, all the battles and all the rescues are lost before they even begin, for if we cannot muster that belief, that strength of heart, of soul, then, how can we be expected to stand when the real heroes are simply small people standing against something greater?

So, yes, the greatest moment of our story had been and gone, the decision made when the words passed the Stranger's lips. The determination that had fluttered about him solidified, encasing his heart and propelling him onward, through the winding streets of Cornucopia and back towards the building that held his beloved. That in truth, held the beloved of so many that it was a wonder none had come to retrieve them before. But fear is strong in the hearts of men, both those that live in this city of extremes and those that come from elsewhere, from cities of lies, and cities built of black and white. Fear is the truest enemy of determination, the weapon that weakens it, that slowly, painfully, destroys it. And although the boy knew fear, and was indeed, at this very moment, afraid, he had taken hold of his fear with both hands and whispered, *'in spite of you'* and it had been the spell to shrink it and bolster his determination.

Most who knew him, who had known the boy he had been, would not have thought him strong enough for the task ahead. How could, after all, anyone be *strong* when their body was visibly weak, restraining them to a chair and the mercy of wheels? But then, strong does not simply mean of body, and there is perhaps far more strength to be found in the mind, and the heart, than in the strongest body in all the worlds. After all, what use is a body of iron and steel if the heart that beats within its rock-hard chest is too weak to carry its shell? And, if I am to speak the whole of the truth, these people never truly knew the Stranger. He was strange if not stranger to them. Withdrawn and quiet, with an ailing body they saw as lesser, wrong, broken. By some twist of luck, or perhaps more accurately, an amazing strength of heart, he never did look at himself as broken. Never saw the chair as anything more or less than his means of transportation, a window to independence.

And now it carried him, up and down cobbled streets, the Regular walking by his side and both their hearts swelling. Hope and determination and the brilliant, shining strength of knowing they were doing what was *right*. And although I would argue, in many cases, that the dichotomy of right and wrong is as complex as defining morality, there is little here that could be perceived as anything but right.

And so, they walked, and so, the Cathedral loomed. Soon they were at the side door the Regular had used and soon after they found the hall the Bartender had told them about. Blackness stretched ahead of them, an absence of everything, an extreme of its own. The Stranger could feel his heart trying to leap out of his chest and the Regular stood stiffly at his side, wondering what ghosts might lurk here to greet her.

No-one, the Bartender had said, used this hall. For it was like walking a road in between your greatest desires and your worst fear and if you took a wrong turn, if your heart doubted or fear choked you, then you would fall down, down, down, and you would drown, drown, drown into nightmares the likes of which no sane mind could conjure. But, the Bartender had said, if you kept your head high and your heart strong and trusted in yourself then, surely, the reward at the end of the road would be worth the risk.

The Stranger and the Regular exchanged a look. They were both worn down, adrift in lives neither had chosen. Both a little unsure as to how their paths had led them here. But in that glance was a promise, a friendship not formed from time and knowledge, but from the quiet companionship born of coming together in a common goal. *Together?* the Stranger's eyes asked. *Together*, the Regular's replied.

And like that, with only the slightest beat of hesitation, they stepped forward into the dark and the unknown.

I could tell you what happened within the corridor of darkness, but there is no way to truly translate what occurred. The pair did not so much traverse as they existed in that darkness and yet, they moved forward. In this extreme of black, this extreme of non-existence, they moved through the magic of Cornucopia, and perhaps came closer to its heart than any had been in a very, very long time.

I could tell you of what they saw—horrors shaped like bloody knives tearing white dresses to shreds, canes of reed made to hurt, cogs that spun and crushed bodies as they did, mouths that existed only to spew hatred—but it would do little to convey what they went through, for you do not know their fear, or, more so, you do not *feel* their fear. You know the

Stranger was hated for who he loved but you do not know the expanse of void opening inside him every time his mother's voice rose and rose. Or perhaps you do, and if that is the case, I would warrant a guess you need no reminder of such horrors. And you know the Regular was once held within this cathedral to idolatry, a sacrifice in a white dress waiting by the altar, blood dripping from wounds that had once been shallow but only grew deeper, but you do not know the way bile rose in her throat, every time a white piece of fabric caught her eye. And if you do, I would guess you need no reminder of that fear, for even if you have conquered it yourself, fear is never so easily entirely eradicated and needs only a spark to rekindle.

So, let me spare those of you who might be hurt by such a tale, and say only to the others that the fear in that corridor had a face, a scent, a taste. It was more than word. And yet, or perhaps more accurately, in spite of that fear, the Stranger and the Regular found their way to a pair of doors. One had a simple streak of red on its surface, and the other was embedded with a constellation of jewels.

There, in that moment, the Regular knew that it was time to face the unfinished business of her childhood, and the Stranger knew that it was time to believe in love like they did in stories.

It might be obvious to you, now, why the Bartender chose to send the Regular here with the Stranger. For helping had never been why the Bartender had sent her. He had sent her for he knew that there are ghosts we must all face before we can find our true paths. The Stranger, meanwhile, needed to think he had help, for he had not yet realised tha: the strength to accomplish all this lay in no-one else but himself.

As the two pushed their respective doors open, a roar of laughter rang through *Moderation* and the Bartender simply smiled, eyes looking far, far beyond his patrons.

THIRTEEN

S leep, soft and gentle. Sleep, deep and troubled. Sleep, with its many faces, fickle as fate or the weather. Sleep was all that echoed behind the Regular's door. She tried to concentrate on its sounds, and not the memories that danced at the edges of her mind. She did not pay attention to the arrangement of bodies wrapped in sleeping bags around the central altar, her gaze avoiding the disturbing figures carved on its surface. She had buried those memories beneath routine and the grinding of cogs, the machinery a part of which she had become. But now that she was free of the latter, the former kept returning in flashes. She had been born here, held here. She would have died here, punishment for the crime of being born on the wrong night.

Or perhaps the *right* night, for to die was said to be a blessing by those who lived here. A blessing to die bleeding as a child, not even ten. Blessing to die in pain, fading a little more each day as food became scarcer and the cuts became deeper, and consciousness was impossible to hold onto. She had watched another die, before her. And another again before that. Every three years they killed one, slowly. It took weeks, and although she barely remembered the first sacrifice, she remembered being afraid. The second, the one branded into her soul, had been a boy who had begged for mercy. For his mother. For food. For love.

She had not begged. She had simply stared when her mother had dressed her in white, a beatific smile on her face—the most terrifying thing she had ever seen—and sat her on the altar. She had been nine. She had understood. They had called it a blessing, but she knew, deep in her soul and in the way of children, that the man who led them spoke lies. There was no god speaking to him. He was the avatar of no powerful spirit. He was but a man with beautiful eyes and a smile made to dazzle and ensorcel, with a tongue so honeyed that it spellbound all those that heard it. This man was not here as a result of an accident. No, he had come here to gain power, to use and manipulate. To get all he wanted. And more, always more. As though people like him were cursed to an eternal want that nothing could ever fulfil, leaving them hollow and frustrated.

As in her memories he sat upon his throne He was not asleep. In a room both too vast and too narrow, he was awake and looking at her. As though he recognised in the woman standing in front of him the girl he had lost so many years ago. She, however, was not looking at him, would *not* look at him. She would not give him this thing that he wanted, the attention he craved. She would not, never again. To her he was nothing, nobody. A ghost. The memory of a ghost. She swallowed her fear and allowed her gaze to land atop the altar.

A young child laid there, and in their white dress and with their long hair she could not judge if it was a boy or a girl. Not that it mattered. They were a little younger than she had been. Perhaps eight, and they clutched the tattered frame of a stuffed toy in their bony, scarred arms, head resting directly on the stone of the altar, cheek stained in their own blood.

The Regular felt fear and anger and hatred and the desperate, choking need to do something, anything.

But above all, she thought of that look exchanged before a dark tunnel, of the determination they shared.

There was no version of this story in which she failed. She was not here alone, though she stood by herself in this cavern of murder and sacrifice. She could feel the Stranger's blue eyes, soft and full of determination; she could see the Bartender's smile, an encouragement on his lips that he had poured to her as a drink red as the sunset against the stained glass of this room.

She took a step forward, flinching as it echoed. But it did not stop her, fear did not consume her. It tried. It clawed at her throat, at her belly, running its ugly hands up and down her arms so they tingled and grew cold. But she stepped on, each stride longer than the last, more purposeful, until she stood by the altar. The child's eyes opened under her gaze, so bright and green against the wanness of their brown skin.

"You will not take him," the man on the throne said, and the Regular heard him stand. But she did not look up. She did not acknowledge him.

He had no power over her.

"You're coming with me," she whispered as she reached down for the child, wrapping him in her arms. He winced and then clung onto her, small hands grasping at her clothes as a terrified sob surged through him.

The man's footsteps were approaching the altar now, not rushed but clipped, as though he knew she could not flee this place.

"You will never leave this place until you give this child back," he said to her. His voice was still beautiful and honeyed, but she heard the words for their meaning, not their sound.

A threat.

His words had always been nothing more than thinly veiled threats meant to bow people to his will. Do this or God will punish you. Do that or God will be angry. She wondered if he had always been here or if he had brought his god from some other monstrous city.

She turned her back to him, the child's face buried in her neck.

"God will not permit you to leave, child. You defied him once, I will not let you defy Him again!" His voice was mounting as though he was preparing for a sermon. Once, when she had been small and frail and had known neither the routine of cogs or the warmth of *Moderation*, she had feared this voice, both awed and terrified by the words it spoke.

But she was no longer a child so easily swayed, and although fear still clawed at her, as it always might around this place, she was not brought low. Not with the child in her arms, not with knowing the Stranger would wait for her beyond the door. And further into the city, the Bartender would be cleaning his glasses and pouring drinks, waiting for them.

Waiting for her to claim the place she was feeling herself drawn to.

The door she had come in through had vanished.

"You will not—"

"Enough." Her voice was like a bell as she spoke, cutting through every part of the silence. "Enough."

She kissed the child's head and then set him down, whispering for him to wait but a moment.

And then, the Regular turned to face her monster. He had not changed, as beautiful and perfect as he had always been, the magic of Cornucopia suiting him well. But in his eyes, she saw something else. Something new. Something so akin to fear that her own almost bled out of her and into him.

"You should have let me go," she told the dark-haired man with skin like alabaster, carved in the image of a beautiful god and imbued with the soul of evil.

"I should have done nothing, girl," he sneered.

Still, none of the sleepers rose. The Regular thought that perhaps it was better this way, that they slept their magicked sleep and woke to a world ready to begin anew. She wondered for a beat if her parents were still here, but she had no time to waste on thoughts that no longer mattered. She had her own family now.

"Your reign ends tonight," she told him, her voice calm.

The man laughed. Mocking. Cruel.

He saw her still as the little girl readied for sacrifice.

He did not see the knife in her pocket, he did not see the shadow of pain, the shadow made solid by belief—belief that held all the magic in this place of worship—turn the insignificant blade into a sword worthy to fell a dragon. He never saw the blow coming.

The Regular would wonder for a long time afterwards, why there had been no blood. Why it had not felt like killing. Nothing had felt real, not with the sleeping bodies around them, not with the magic of her own belief so raw around her, a magic she had not known she could wield. She would wonder about that too. Had there been magic? When she had pulled the sword out it had been nothing more than a knife, but the man was dead, his face frozen in a scream he'd had no right to voice. She would never know if the sword she had seen had been real or not. It didn't matter.

The man was gone.

The tension around her snapped, though she knew the sleepers would not wake yet. The little boy stared at her. She could have told him his parents would wake soon, that they would be different, that they would remember how to love him. But instead she asked: "Do you want to come with me?" and he nodded his small head, curls bouncing with the motion.

She took him in her arms, and the door was there again, outlined in silver light. The door, come for her now that her business was done.

The child held tightly onto her and she allowed herself a smile as she pushed the door open onto their freedom.

FOURTEEN

There was darkness beyond the door, and at first the Stranger thought that it was all-encompassing. But a single candle burned as bright as a single flame might. Around it, the room took shape: plush furniture and a luxurious bed. Jewellery and elegant fabrics draped on every surface. It was a gauntlet for the wheelchair, but the Stranger had become used to this throughout the years, knowing too well how keen the world was to make itself awkward for him. Still, he found his way, through the maze of clothes and cushions, to the bed near which the candle rested.

He saw him, then, the boy who haunted his dreams and waking thoughts alike.

Golden hair spilt on sapphire pillows, a halo for a face of perfect beauty. Only there was a tightness to that face, a frown creasing its brows. The lips formed a thin line, and there was something gaunt to him. Drained. He wore little, only silken pants and a sheaf of gauzy voile around his chest, but the heavy jewellery he wore told a story all their own.

Wide bands of gold like prison cuffs encircled his neck and wrists. They did not bind him and yet the Stranger felt as though their weight held him down all the same.

He reached out, afraid, and let his fingers graze the Idol's cheek in the way it had a hundred times before in secret shared moments, tucked away from the world. His skin was as soft and smooth as always but felt at once both cold and feverish. Fingers trailed down to the collar at his neck, the thick band of gold that looked as though it wanted to strangle him.

The Idol did not wake, not even as the Stranger slid from his chair to the edge of the bed, sinking into the soft mattress as he drew closer to the other boy. Silence reigned over the room, with only the candle for company. Not even the softest of snores could be heard from the other side of the door to the main hall. The main hall full of people that would grab, and claw, and claim, and refuse to let go. He needed to wake the Idol before they realised he was here, for they would stop them from escaping this nightmare of opulence.

He pulled himself close enough to lean his head against the Idol's chest, black locks on pale skin, the candle keeping the shadows from swallowing them both. There was only them in the world. Only them. Not even the world remained, the glow of the candle strong enough only for the two boys on the bed.

It had been in such a moment that they had been found. Lips to lips, fingers entwined, and all had been revealed. Every careful deception unveiled, every secret wordlessly spilled, staining their future in the red of blood and loss and pain. It had happened in the snap of fingers, so brief, so unavoidable. It had taken hours. Days. Months. Speeches and punishments. It had taken everything. And yet here they were. Just them. Alone at last with only the memory of a flame keeping the darkness at bay.

The Stranger wondered what would happen if the candle went out, if the darkness would swallow them and everything would simply...end. Was there a monster hiding, quietly waiting to devour them? Or would nothing happen? Would they simply find themselves with no light to guide them?

"Wake up," he whispered, barely daring to raise his voice. "Wake up, my love."

The Idol did not so much as stir and his skin now felt clammy under the Stranger's touch, twisting his insides with worry. What had they done to him? What spell had they cast, what drug had they given him? And how was he to counter it?

Like in the stories, he thought. They had once both been avid readers after all, eager to write their own faery tale.

"I love you," he whispered, the three words they had uttered to each other but once before their parents had come crushing their lives, ruining everything. "I love you," he repeated, and then again, a third time, as though it was a spell. "I love you."

Lips met lips; soft flesh gently touched. A peck, really, and yet so much more. It was rain on a scalding day, coming first as a scent and then a shiver through the air, culminating in a blissful shudder of cool. It was a fire-raising crescendo as it found new kindling to burn, crackling and popping until the flames danced high as a racing heart. It was so small a thing. It had been so long denied.

It was everything.

The Idol's eyes fluttered open, eyelids heavy with gold powder as he was dragged out of his stupor. His eyes were unfocused. But when they found the Stranger, they cleared at the very impossibility of what he was seeing. The Stranger, with his soft, sad smile so full of love. The Stranger who, to the Idol, was no stranger at all.

Silence stretched, both boys muted by incredulity. They looked at one another, blue eyes lost in green ones, gazes filled with hope and love and longing and all the things that no words were made to say, as though the experience of such things was too precious, too intimate to be translated. There was magic in the air around them, the same magic that had woken the Idol with a kiss, that had gifted power to repetition—three times for the charm, three times for luck. It was the simplest of all magic, the oldest perhaps. The magic of love. And although here it applied to love romantic, the magic of love does not discriminate between family or friends or lovers, keen instead to manifest in different ways.

"You came," the Idol said, the first words to shatter the silence.

Something caught in the Stranger's throat, a breath like a laugh that broke onto a sob.

"Of course."

Whatever had come over the Idol the day before when he had seen him tangled in the crowd was gone, his eyes full of recognition, awake to him if not the world beyond their candlelight. The Stranger would not have minded if time stopped now, trapping them in this bubble of togetherness.

"All this way?" the Idol asked, one hand moving to cup the Stranger's face. "After everything?"

There were tears in the Stranger's eyes.

"Always."

A bold promise for a boy who did not believe in faery tale endings. But here he was, the Idol's hand on his face, his own fingers dancing in golden locks. He had found him. Against all hope. He had been told he was a fool, that there was no way he could find him and if he did, he could never come home. But the Stranger had not had a home since the day his secret had been discovered, for how could any place be *home* when it did not welcome all of you?

The Idol's smile was taut and tired though genuine. He looked a little lost even as he glanced past the Stranger and at the darkened room.

"I don't really remember how I got here," he admitted. "I don't really understand why I'm here. It all made sense until... Until I woke just now. I can still remember what it felt like to be here but it's all... It's all gone now." He passed a hand over his face, slowly sitting up on the bed. His jewellery was like music on the wind as he moved and both of them winced at the sudden, unexpected noise, so loud in the silence. Even the candle seemed to gutter for a second.

"It doesn't matter now," the Stranger said, though his own anxiety clawed at him. "We can leave now."

"I feel like I can't. Like I shouldn't."

The Stranger swallowed his reaction, swallowed the fear. His heart was racing. Hope was wavering, an inescapable feeling of helplessness washing over him. Had this all been for nothing? Would the other boy choose to forget and stay? To keep this place the world had made for him alone? Or was it that the world had made *him* for this place? Did it even matter which way things had transpired?

"You can. Of course, you can. You can come with me. We can be together."

Conflicted green eyes met desperate blue ones. The Stranger felt his smile falter and tears stick to his lashes. Fingers alongside his, twining in an achingly familiar motion he hardly dared to return.

"Together? Can we really do that? Where would we even go?"

"Anywhere? There are plenty of places where no-one will care who we love. I've been to them whilst looking for you. I know there is a place for us somewhere, small and cosy and *ours*. Like we always wanted."

They looked at one another, these two boys who had lost each other. One who had run away and the other who had broken free to follow, to seek, to rescue. Rescue from himself, from the pain that had grown so large as to swallow him whole. Both sitting on an opulent bed, surrounded by darkness and riches, with eyes only for one another.

"Will it work?" The Idol asked, and he sounded scared.

"If we do it together, it will. I know we can make this work," the Stranger said, holding out a hand to the boy he loved. The boy he needed in his life.

There was another pause, another moment when time stretched infinite and impossible, and then the Idol placed his hand in the Stranger's.

"I love you," he said simply, and it was answer enough. It said everything that needed to be said.

And it was magic. A spell cast, a spell broken. There was a sound like a crack but quiet, and yet loud as a gun, and the golden bracelets fell from the Idol's wrists, the matching collar at his throat toppling onto the bed with barely a sound. But to the place around them, it was like a wakeup call.

The candle guttered out and before either of them had finished their gasp of surprise, bright, blinding light flooded the room. And beyond the door... Sounds of waking. People moving. Like a fevered panic.

"We need to go!" the Stranger exclaimed, all but throwing himself into his chair as the Idol scrambled to his feet.

They moved without hesitation, a duo caught once and torn apart and keen to be free at last. Beyond the door voices grew closer but already the Stranger was at the door he had come in through, grasping the handle.

The door did not move.

The voices from outside reached them now, calling for the Idol, fanatic and fevered. Deafening. Panic seized the young men's hearts as the door resisted them still and the other door started to crack open. Soon they would be swarmed. Soon they would be torn apart. *Again.* The Idol reached for the door handle too, seeking to add his strength in their bid to freedom, but no sooner had both their hands touched the handle that the door swung outward. They did not pause to marvel at the magic, did not hesitate as they fled into the corridor even as the other door came open and the cries of worshippers watching their makeshift god flee dogged their escape.

The door slammed behind them, locking away the past. They would have been hand in hand if the Stranger had not had need of both his to wheel himself forward. He had never been awfully fond of being pushed and the Idol was too dizzy now to offer much help. But they looked at each other, and there were smiles on their faces.

"Thought you two were never going to make it out," a voice said, and the Stranger turned, relief washing over him as he saw the Regular, a small child held in her arms and a new determination in her eyes. "So, shall we get out of here once and for all?"

The two young men did not need asking twice.

FIFTEEN

The night was dark and bright all at once, as can only happen within cities, with the darkness above held at bay by dazzling man-made light. The stars were not in hiding behind clouds anymore, though still mostly invisible to those who walked the streets of Cornucopia, blinded to the lights above by those around them, keeping them both safe and trapped all at once. Three streets away from where our group walked out from the Cathedral of Idols, one of said lights guttered out. When the sun would rise and pierce the fog, the dying of that single bulb would be marked by a body, face down on the pavement. Irrelevant to our story, yes, but proof indeed of Cornucopia's callous nature. On a night that should have been for celebration, the city saw no harm in letting its citizens fall prey to the most undesirable of its creations.

But for our group the lights stayed on, and the streets they walked were clear of trouble. It was, after all, the least they deserved. They attracted many stares: that of the curious and the judging, that of the confused and the wondering. They did, after all, make for a rather strange quartet: a boy in a wheelchair, a girl with a face still partially painted with grease, a child in a white gown, and another boy with bare feet and sheer clothing that left little to the imagination. But none of them cared.

And why should they? Had they not, after all, accomplished their mission? What did it matter to them that they stood out as strange and unusual in a city that itself was strange and unusual?

Still, even as people stared, they made way for them, and some even looked away from their gazes, frightened to meet them. They felt something about the group that unsettled them, a freedom, a lack of tether holding them fast to the city. They were not believers; they were not worshippers. There was no excess or denial for them. They did not bow the knee to opulence or buried their faces in abstinence. They did not wear matching riches or pauper's robes, did not walk with the single-minded purpose of the cogs working inside the machine. Their feet were unhurried now that the rain had stopped, their faces painted not with awe but relief and laughter.

Some amongst the ones they passed knew that if they looked into their eyes, they would see the madness of freedom, of unbelief, of *moderation*. But to them, what shone in their eyes was not madness, but love, happiness, the light that had been smothered by a weight at last diminished.

There was an ending in the air, but it did not come alone. Unlike the body three streets away, this ending was no full stop. Only a semicolon, a break on the page as the storyteller catches their breath. It was an ending that came with magic, the soft whispering of a door closing, propelling ten others open.

Truly, there were *beginnings* in the air.

The group did not speak of where they were headed, for the two that led knew without words where they were going. To where the chapter of this story had begun, to a place at once familiar and strange, a place that never changed and yet was not always the same.

They walked, and silence was no longer their companion. They spoke of nothing and everything: of cities where hours were reserved to turn off all the light so the people could bathe in the starlight, of places where the horizon seemed to stretch and stretch and stretch, never obscured by a single mountain or tree or building. They spoke of machines that made wonders and wonders turned to machines, and in the Regular's arms, the boy listened with fascination, watched the city around him with eyes full of wonder. He was no longer afraid.

At last, they turned off the main streets and into the smaller, winding alleys that lead to *Moderation*. Neither the Stranger nor the Regular was surprised to find the place open, even this late at night. The child was asleep in the Regular's arms and the Idol was fighting his own tiredness, but here they were at last, their destination, the final rest before the ending.

The bar was empty and quiet inside, candlelight burning low, but one table was ready: five chairs, three glasses and a mug of hot chocolate waiting for them. And on the fifth chair, a soft smile playing on his lips, the Bartender waited.

SIXTEEN

The Regular and the Stranger told their story at once briefly and in great detail. As they spoke, the Bartender listened and the Boy fell asleep with his head in the Regular's lap as the Idol leaned his head on the Stranger's shoulder, eyes half closed and basking in the feeling of closeness. The Bartender listened with a smile, eyes lost in the grain of the table's wood, drawing patterns with his fingers among the stains. There was both so little and so much to say, but time did not seem to pass as they spoke, even the clock on the back wall strangely steady in its lack of advance. It was as though their victory had frozen Cornucopia; time unable to move as the city struggled to pull itself back together.

They drank a beautifully green alcohol served in glasses shaped like water lilies, a touch of excess in this plain setting for it was, after all, a celebration. The Bartender had seen many such celebrations, though each came in different shapes and with varied visages. Some had not been so complete, and the smiles had held tears and sometimes tears had held smiles. But always, always there had been the green alcohol, for luck and fortune and the future ahead. And always he had sat in this very chair, at this very table, drawing endless patterns in the wood as he listened to the stories of freedom won and freedom gained.

And then, when the stories were told, people went on their way and rare were the times where he would see them again, for their paths usually took them away from Cornucopia. Tonight was a particularly late celebration, and although the Stranger did have a hotel room to his name, it was far from here and the exhaustion that permeated his four guests was surprisingly catching. So, as the stories and drinks were finished, he offered them all to stay in the rooms above. The Regular had been rather shocked to hear that the Bartender had rooms for board above but for answer he gave her only a smile. There would be time for questions in the morning, once well-earned rest had been gotten.

He watched them stumble off upstairs, knowing *Moderation* would guide them to their doors, and he felt a slight pang in his chest. He had known the Regular for a long time, since before she had been old enough to drink though she had come by every day to do so, and every day he would gift her a glass of some juice and promise her wonders from it, smiling as he made her describe the taste in emotions. She had once drunk a juice so sour that her entire face had scrunched up in a scowl and she had told him the juice tasted like old people who put others down because they had failed to become what they were meant to be.

That day, when he had watched her saunter back off to her shift, he had wished she would stay. That she would open her eyes to the truth of Cornucopia and escape its clutches. And now that she had, the Bartender realised he would miss her. She would surely leave, most did, and *Moderation* would feel a little bit lonely without her coming in and out on the daily.

The thoughts followed him back to the bar, still empty, though it was only a matter of time until someone found their way here, and he set about tidying the table. He was humming a song to himself and had just finished cleaning the glasses, when he heard soft footsteps behind him. He was rather startled when he turned, to find the Regular standing in the doorway, framed by the light of the stairs behind. She had washed her face and her hands and stood in nothing but her trousers and a tank-top, her feet in thick socks.

"You should be asleep," he told her, not meeting her deep, intense gaze as it lingered on him.

"Couldn't exactly go to sleep knowing there was still some work to be done," she replied, nodding towards the table where they had sat. Indeed, rings of moisture still covered it, and the bruised remnants of a spilt drink stood out amongst them.

"This is not your work," the Bartender told her, a note of hopeful wonder in his voice.

"Isn't it?" she asked. There was a spring in her step as she came behind the bar, grabbed a cleaning cloth and slung it over her shoulder in the way he often did. "I thought I was free to decide where I belonged?"

"I imagined you would leave," the Bartender replied, his eyes not quite on her as he smiled.

"And go where? This is the only place I've ever known. Plus," a casual shrug as she reached for a cleaning product and headed to the offending table, "if all of us who learn better leave, then who will be left to teach the rest of the city?"

"Me," the Bartender replied simply.

"Sure, but wouldn't it be easier if there was more than just you? I mean, I'm not saying I'll be much use with your fancy drinks straight away but..." Another shrug, though the fear that he might send her away was clear in her eyes. "I'm sure there are plenty of things I could do around here."

"Yes, yes, I think there could be," the Bartender replied, smile growing on his lips, the dance of his butterfly hands accelerating as he carried on tidying. "I think I could get used to having someone else around. But what about the boy you brought back?"

"I guess that'll be up to him, won't it? He could stay with us or go with the boys or find somewhere else in the city. I don't know, but I always did wish I'd had a younger sibling."

The Bartender chuckled softly at that. "Then I suppose he can stay too, if he so wishes. Though I expect the three of us might make for a very odd family."

"That's the only kind of family I want," the Regular replied without missing a beat.

She turned, then, to face the Bartender and he, too, in a rare moment that carried so much weight, turned his gaze fully to her. Their eyes met for less than a heartbeat, but in that breath the Regular knew she was home. Properly. Fully.

It was as though the puzzle of her life had come together and now she could see how to fill in the blanks.

A breath later and the door opened, admitting in a pair of women, their arms interlinked, and their cloaks drawn tight as they headed for one of the back tables. Without missing a beat, the Bartender began to serve their drinks and the Regular was there, taking the glasses from the other side of the bar. As easily as that, despite the late hour and how tired all parties were, they found their rhythm together.

SEVENTEEN

The Stranger and the Idol said their farewell to the Bartender at *Moderation* later the next day, after sharing a meal and more drinks and resting enough to feel up to travelling. The Regular had done some shopping for them and now the Idol stood in a beautiful outfit matching the cut of the Stranger's though it came in a hue of blues that matched the Stranger's eyes. The Regular had insisted on accompanying them all the way to the airship landing that sat high up above the city. The Stranger was a charged man, his whole countenance alive, and the smile he'd been wearing when he exited the Cathedral still bright on his lips.

They stood atop the tall structure that was the airship dock, Cornucopia sprawling at their feet. The city looked somewhat lesser from this far up, all its traps and nasty parts hidden beneath fog and sunlight, and perhaps also behind the spell of *Moderation* cast on the three as they waited for the airship to be ready for its passengers. The Regular's eyes were wide with wonders whilst the boys stood close, hands interlaced, everything about them revealing how they felt for the other.

"I can't even begin to guess where *Moderation* is from here," the Regular said, squinting through the window at the city below.

"Are you sure you want to stay?" the Stranger asked her, not for the first time, and by now it rang of formality more than anything else.

As she had done every other time, the Regular shook her head, returning to staring at the inside of the docks, at the high vaulted ceiling that gave onto empty sky, at the brutal simplicity of the platforms that extended out and where ships were docked. She looked at the ornately dressed staff whose eyes were filled with awe as they turned to whisper prayers to the ships, and she saw the severe outfits of the security team that walked around, offering no prayer to anything for their belief lay in strength and strength alone.

The station was, in many ways, like a small recreation of the city below, a taste of what was to come for travellers and tourists and those who came searching for their place here.

"What will you do now?" the Stranger asked the Regular as she returned her attention to him and the Idol.

"Bartender's got a lot to teach me," she said with a smile. "And who knows, maybe one day I'll be the one pouring drinks to some lost soul to send them on their way." She paused, eyes a little dreamy. "I think I'd like that. Cornucopia is a hundred kinds of messed up but... it's home. The only one I've ever known and the only one I want. If I can make even a little bit of a difference to some people, then I want to try. What about you two?"

The Stranger and the Idol exchanged a glance, one that spoke of a night spent less in sleep and more in talking, in hurried plans and then the decision made, finally slipping into slumber beside one another.

"We're going to be travelling for a bit. Until we find somewhere that's right for us to settle," the Stranger said.

The Regular smiled, and although there was a hint of a question on her lips, she never let it out. She would not have had the chance to, either way, for an announcement rang throughout the station and easy as that, it was time for the Stranger and the Idol to go. The Regular felt a pang at watching them go, knowing she was unlikely to ever see them again and it was well known that letters in between the Fractured Cities were lost more often than they were found.

They hugged, the Regular and the Stranger holding on particularly tightly. After all, they knew so much about each other now that, whether they wanted it or not, a part of the other would always live inside their heart. Even if memories were to fade, they knew in that embrace that they would never truly forget the person they had overcome such ordeal alongside.

Then, without another word, for words could not possibly convey all that they were feeling, the three parted ways. The Stranger and the Idol boarded the airship and headed for their cabin, keen to be alone, to get to hold each other away from prying eyes they never knew whether to trust or not. The Regular stood on the platform and watched the airship pull away, grateful beyond words that the young men did not come to the bridge to wave at her for she doubted her heart could take yet another farewell. She would be happy enough remembering them heading inside the airship, close and smiling, the feel of their embraces still warm around her. She watched until the airship was but a speck on the horizon and then turned away. After all, she had errands to run before she returned to *Moderation*. Before she returned home.

On the airship, the young men sat together on their large bed, heads leaning against one another, eyes closed as they simply let the enormity of what they had been through fall away. Every breath, every second that passed, they could feel Cornucopia diminish, as if the city's talons had still been reaching for them and at last, they were free. They found each other's hands on the bed, and then their lips met and there was the soft sound of startled laughter when something is so much more than you remembered it being. After that, all there was for them was each other and the soft rocking of the ship. And beyond that, beyond the bright sky above the clouds, tucked in another city, waited their tomorrow.

Alek L. Cristea is a trans, gay, witch who writes the queer YA SFF he wanted—and needed—to read when he was a teen.

When not scribbling words he's found reading, playing video games, or engaged with one of his many other hobbies (which he seems to keep accumulating over the years).

Alek has been making worlds up since he can remember, first for his toys to inhabit, and then in his head.

Even now these stories get downloaded (if only) to paper, all that daydreaming takes up an impressive amount of processing power— meaning you can bet he always leaves the laundry in the drum and never folds the bedding. (Cooking though - that never gets forgotten, because that's a magic all its own!)

He lives with his three cats and his not-quite-husband and is desperately attempting to grow more than weeds in their small garden (he manages a decent crop of strawberries each year in spite of everything). At least the bees are entertained.

Find more about his writing on his website (https://aleklcristea.com/)